BASE CASE

Julian Rathbone

BASE CASE

Michael Joseph

London

First published in Great Britain by Michael Joseph Ltd
44 Bedford Square, London WC1
1981

© 1981 by Julian Rathbone

ISBN 0 7181 1993 2

Printed and bound in Great Britain by
Redwood Burn Ltd., Trowbridge and Esher.

Author's Note

Readers of *The Euro-Killers* will
remember that Brabt lies on the
coast between Holland and Belgium.
    Clearly the Virtue Islands are
also imagined — how else could
they be in that part of the
Atlantic at present occupied by
the Canaries?

I

THE 707 trundled through the skies on communications beams as fixed and predictable as tramlines. That at least is the illusion which converts spaces into a medium as supportive as water and safer — you can't drown in air. Twenty thousand feet above the Vignemale, the highest mountain in the French Pyrenees, the captain reset the controls to tilt the nose on to the long descent towards Madrid, and the vapour trail took a slight dog-leg to the right. Below, the leader of a short daisy-chain of climbers glanced up from the piton he had just lodged in a crevice before edging his cramponned feet a yard up the iced rock-face. He reflected that he at least was on solid ground.

In the plane a radio crackled and the third officer began to scribble on his pad.

A metre or so behind him water spiralled round a stainless steel bowl. Jan Argand momentarily glimpsed his face in the dark mirror above the sink, and flinched away. Since his illness the consciousness that lay behind his eyes no longer felt at home with the mask that lay in front of it. The heavy and high-arched eyebrows, the beak-like nose and deep lines were a surprise when he bothered to take them in. Always he hoped to see a face younger, more vulnerable, happier, and above all more familiar.

He opened the metal door, caught a glimpse of one of the stewardesses' tiny galleys, and then passed grimly through the first-class cabin and so back to his seat in tourist. The first class was filled with Arabs — an oil sheikh and his entourage. Argand,

7

Commissioner Argand of the Brabt Police, was irritated by them, and not just because he would have been travelling first but for them — he resented the bland politeness accorded them by everyone in Europe from Eurocrats to air hostesses. One of the latter was sitting on the arm of a seat from which a princeling not more than fifteen years old was chatting her up. The service in tourist had been appalling.

Beyond the partition the humming tube was packed and, in spite of the draughty air-conditioning, smelt flat and stale. At the front there were six more Arabs — three bodyguards and three women. The bodyguards were clearly armed — in contravention of the regulations. Argand detested law-breaking and most of all when it was carried out flagrantly by the privileged. The women were in black with obscene black masks on their noses. Were they servants? Or just women? There was no telling.

The rest of the passengers were for the most part Dutch, Belgian, Brabanter families taking advantage of the first off-season rates for a late holiday in the Virtue Islands. They were large, blond, overweight and noisy, their children pasty-faced and ill-mannered. Then there were immigrant workers — poorly dressed, cheerful, but pale from a year spent doing the jobs northern Europeans prefer to have done for them. Finally a sprinkling of the well-to-do who never pay for their air tickets — the businessmen, technocrats and bureaucrats who had been displaced by the Arabs. Most of these cut themselves off from their alien surroundings by busying themselves with papers taken from black, steel-framed document cases, as much a part of their uniforms as the British-style suits they all wore. There were two or three academics as well — on their way, Argand had gathered, to a literary conference to be held in Las Guavas, capital of the islands.

One of these, a woman, now leaned across his path, her mouth at the level of his genitals. She was talking briskly to the man across the gangway from her.

"Look," she was saying, "you can't dismiss a fact by saying it's Marxist. The dominant mode of production *does* affect all social relations, that's a fact. You can't run away from it."

She looked up at Argand and pulled back. Something about her face made him pause. She had dark brown eyes beneath heavy unplucked brows, looked as if she would be stocky when standing up. No make-up, a pleasant open sort of face. Argand felt a sense of dread — he knew the face, knew it from long ago, could not now place it. And the association had been an uncomfortable one, one best forgotten, forgotten indeed until now, when all that remained of it was this sharp touch of dread.

On the pull-down shelf in front of her she too had a small document case and a book, a glossy paperback with a pencil lying beside it. The book was French — *Pour une Théorie de la Production Littéraire* by Pierre Macherey. But she had been speaking Brabanter, the dialect of Brabt, the small semi-autonomous corner of Europe where Argand was, or had been, a senior policeman.

Her face tilted up at him. Waited. She wanted him to pass.

"I'm sorry," he murmured, and swung himself on down the vinyl-lined tube.

"And the relationship between reader and text is a social one," he heard her say, unaware that she had also felt the presence of something from the past, but for her the moment had been touched with bile, the after-taste of a hate now dulled by time.

At his seat he stooped, glanced through the window on the other side of his neighbour. Beyond and beneath the trembling silver edge of the wing, ochre hills scarred by erosion stretched to purple mountains. The Valley of the Ebro. His neighbour smiled shyly up at him, wriggled deeper into his seat as if he had been trespassing on Argand's territory in the latter's absence. Argand picked up his document case which he had left behind him and put it across his knees, unlocked the catches. He breathed in deeply, his large nostrils flaring, let the flat, recycled air sigh noisily out of

9

his lungs, and pulled out the paper that lay on top.

"Project Achilles has been long in the making," he read for the third time, for he had nothing else to read, "but recent events in Afghanistan, the deployment of medium-range nuclear missiles in eastern Europe, and numerous other provocations have made it increasingly clear that its initial conception as a relevant response to communist expansion in Africa was a correct one — only the level of this response needs now to be updated . . ." His attention drifted.

His neighbour's brown hand lay at the end of the shared arm-rest between them. Argand noticed the long fingers clenching and relaxing, clenching so the small-boned knuckles paled beneath the brown skin. Involuntarily he looked up and his glance caught black eyes in bloodshot whites staring sidelong at him. They flinched away and came back. We are too close to each other, thought Argand — indeed he could just catch a hint of stale spices on the man's breath.

"Not long now, I mean not long before we are making our stop at Madrid."

The Indian, if that was what he was, spoke English, had earlier established that it was a tongue they shared, had offered Argand a mildly pornographic magazine in that language. Argand had not hidden his distaste and had hoped thereby to secure his privacy.

"Twenty-one minutes and fifteen seconds. My stepfather gave me this. It is very good I think." This was said with a pride innocent and inoffensive. The watch was a gold Rolex Oyster, non-digital, presumably clockwork.

Soon the low-slung engines became insistent, the horizons seemed nearer, were more tilted. Chimes came from the public address system and Argand reached for his seat belt as a man's voice — the captain's? — made an announcement in Spanish. It was a long announcement. More than the routine affair of fasten

10

your seat belts, no more smoking. Argand waited, head on one side, for the English version and was aware that his neighbour's stress had become acute. The Indian's fist was now clenched, his face pale beneath the brownish pigments; even the smell seemed more noticeable, sourer, more animal. At last the announcement came in English.

"Ladies and gentlemen your attention please, your attention please. We are now approaching Barajas Airport, the airport of Madrid. Our estimated time of arrival is thirteen thirty-five local time and the temperature at Barajas is twenty-eight degrees centigrade and the sun is shining. I have to advise you that following an information from ground-to-air control at Barajas our stop there will be longer than the scheduled fifty minutes. Passengers for Santa Caridad are advised that they will be asked to leave the plane at Barajas, that their baggage will be offloaded and rechecked, and that everything will be transferred to another plane. Líneas Aèreas de las Islas, LADI, apologize for any inconvenience this may cause and we assure our respected clients that all will be done possible to minimize any delays that may arrive. Thank you. Messieurs et Mesdames . . ."

The Indian clenched his hands together in his lap, rolled his eyes sideways at Argand.

"I think there may be some trouble," he said.

"Perhaps. Perhaps there is." Argand felt a momentary sympathy for his companion. The man was obviously in a cold funk — almost Argand envied him, envied the hold he appeared to have on life. "I'm sure they'll do all they can to minimize whatever danger we are in."

"Oh yes. I am certain of that. Of course." The dark face turned away, looked out of the window. The plane tilted and Argand could see they were still over high ground, mountains even, brown rocks, dried yellow grassland, forest. The Guadarramas perhaps?

11

The Indian looked back, again caught Argand's eyes full on, too close.

"You are going on to Santa Caridad?" he asked.

"Oh yes. I am going to Santa Caridad," said Argand, and then abruptly turned back to the papers on his knee, unwilling to continue a conversation that was pointless, even distasteful. He leafed over pages already familiar, passed on to the last.

"The Base on Santa Caridad, linked with the Space Detection and Tracking Systems (SPADATS) on Mount San Cristóbal, will thus be the boss of our Atlantic Shield against communist aggression, our Shield of Achilles. We welcome you to our team of dedicated experts, strong in our united knowledge that the work we do is sanctified by the cause of freedom and the future, indeed survival of mankind. God Bless Us All. Sam Peters." Who is Sam Peters again? Argand asked himself, and leafed back to the beginning. Oh yes. Chief Liaison Officer. He looked up, but unseeingly. A grim smile touched the corner of his mouth — he had not approved the rhetoric, but the content was right enough, yes indeed, he had no reservations at all about Project Achilles.

Restlessly he pushed aside the introductory leaflet, and fidgeted amongst the maps, plans, and guides to Santa Caridad that lay beneath. Then the insistently buzzing conversations around him caught his attention and he snapped the case shut.

Strangers who had maintained separateness for two hours, ever since they had embarked at Amsterdam, were now searching, almost desperately, for some point of contact with the person it seemed they might, just possibly, die next to. The man across the gangway, middle-aged, presumably a businessman, leant across.

"It's a bomb I expect. Well, let's keep our fingers crossed. Not necessarily a bomb, but a bomb-scare."

"Yes?" said Argand. "Do you think so?"

"I think so. That's why they want everyone off and all the

12

baggage rechecked. Mark my words. It's those Arabs, I'm sure of it. My secretary wanted to book the next flight when she'd discovered they'd taken over the first class. But I've always put the firm first and now this happens."

"It's more likely to be Virtudian separatists."

But the businessman rambled on with his own theories.

Eventually Argand contrived to disengage himself from the bonhomie of the doomed. Dread like a block of ice settled somewhere behind his diaphragm. There might be a bomb. Yes indeed there might. But no need to suppose Arabs were the target nor that Virtudian separatists were the terrorists. There were people, there were *those* who would sleep a lot better, whose interests would be far more secure if the plane Commissioner Argand was on was blown out of the sky.

The silver wing tilted again, and again the chimes came over the rising whine of the reversed engines. This time it was the safety belts, the cigarettes to be dowsed, but with an extra warning, surely not routine, that there was no cause for alarm, a perfectly normal landing was expected. The mountains gave way to parched parkland, burnt up pasture between small evergreen oaks, a glimpse of a large house, a palace surrounded by woods, and a trickle of a river at the bottom of a ravine. Then high-rise apartment blocks still five, ten miles off, but on a skyline far closer than any they had seen since they left Amsterdam in a grey drizzle. The plane levelled and the mountains, distant and higher now, reappeared. Argand thought: this is not how I should have chosen to go, not in this ridiculous plastic and metal tube filled with stale air, recycled tobacco smoke, intestinal gases provoked by the foul food, listening to muted strings playing a Schubert melody over a reggae beat. A memory flashed across his inner vision, a memory of a white tern hovering above foam-flecked wavelets, green and then blue, and then there was the touch and rumble of wheels on

13

concrete and the airport buildings flashing by, slowing, slowing almost to a walking pace as the aircraft turned and replaced them with low ochre hills, the nearest crowned with a large black cut-out bull, high-horned, well-sexed, and the legend *Osborne Brandy*. The engines cut back to a murmur and above the noise they heard the urgent two-toned summons of sirens as fire engines, ambulances, and police cars raced across the tarmac towards them.

The Indian unbuckled, stood up, took a case much like Argand's from the rack above his head, and slipped into it his glossy magazine with its cover girl, a red-head in dark stockings and nothing else.

"It looks like we made it," he said, and he wiped the sweat from under his ear.

Large black cars wafted the sheikh and his entourage to safety in a matter of seconds. With far less urgency the rest of them were bussed across the airfield to the terminals, herded up steep slopes cocooned in extendable flexi-walls, pushed into a wide, bleak room furnished with low plastic-covered benches. A low promontory pushed into the middle, bulged at the end into a circle, supported a conveyor belt. Policemen, some in grey uniforms, some in green, all armed and some with machine carbines, stood across the glass doors that yet separated them from the parterres beyond — two of them even blocked off the passageway up which they had come.

Moments of indecision and doubt passed like small eternities. The gossip level rose — that there had been a bomb on board, in somebody's luggage perhaps, was clearly the consensus. Argand looked around him, aware of the smell of stale spice again, and found the Indian behind him. He had now pulled a woven light blue jacket over the white shirt and cravat he had been wearing on the plane. His black hair combed back in waves from his forehead glistened in the twilight of the hall they were in — transit lounge,

14

customs shed, whatever it was. He smiled up ingratiatingly at Argand.

"Still we are living in one piece," he said. "I mean not yet in little bits."

Argand turned away, found his nose was almost touching the top of a dark girl's head, the Brabanter girl — well woman really, she was well over thirty — who had prompted a dread-filled memory from the past.

" 'Knowledge without action is not knowledge'," she was saying to the man she had been talking to earlier. "That is always the temptation. The temptation and the justification for acts of terrorism," and with the slogan that had been air-sprayed on countless walls the memory became sharper. '68. Argand, then Deputy Commissioner for Public Order. Student riots. Twelve years ago, her name was . . . something beginning with B.

The conveyor clanked, stopped, clanked again and settled down to a steady rumble. A large suitcase, another, then a procession of them mingled with the brown paper parcels and sacks tied with string that belonged to the immigrant workers ambled down the promontory into the hall, swung round the bulge at the end, and so back out again — those that hadn't been identified and plucked off as they passed. The crowd pressed in towards them, Argand felt pressure behind, perhaps from the Indian. He saw his own black leather grip go by, tried to squeeze past the pair in front, and then felt his document case, still held in his left hand, snagging on something, someone behind him. His black leather grip slid by, just out of reach, and at just that second the English businessman a few yards away said: "The bloody fools, they haven't checked it yet. The bomb could still be amongst that lot," and there was a sudden surge away from the conveyor, a surge that became a stampede. Argand felt his document case dragged from him, he let go, and with the people behind him pushing for dear life tripped and fell to his knees. Someone screamed, then another. People pushed past and over him and he lost his hat, saw it trodden on. He was angry now, not frightened. He stood up, elbows out, braced his back against the flow and announced firmly in a loud voice, first in Brabanter then in English, that there was no need to panic, that panic would help no one, that he was sure the authorities knew what they were doing.

At that moment the bomb went off. The blast hit him in the back like a weighted sack, knocking the breath out of him, and the thought flashed across his mind: that was meant for me. Not for the Arabs.

II

FOUR days earlier, in his old-fashioned but luxurious office in Wilhelmstras, Wotan Prinz, Secretary for Civic Affairs in the semi-autonomous Province of Brabt, had pulled Argand's medical report out of his pending tray, lit his large and noisome pipe, and settled down to make up his mind about what to do with the Honest Commissioner. Rank smoke floated about his large head, his heavy lip drooped moistly beneath the pipe stem, his fingers, already podgy, leafed through the reports. He nodded occasionally, grunted, sometimes made small but self-important notes in the margins with a slim gold pencil. Thus for the best do those who know best dispose of things.

"From Doctor/Licentiate Klaus Rebb, Brabt State Hospital, Psychiatric Wing, 20 August 1980. Ref. Commissioner Jan Argand.

"Subject was admitted on 7 April 1980 at 17.35 hours at the request of the Department of Civic Affairs. He was clearly under severe mental strain, suffering from delusions and hallucinations. It was soon established that moods of depression characterized by refusal to co-operate or communicate were alternating with outbursts of violent and aggressive activity. He was immediately sedated and placed under restraint.

"In the next two days, consultation with officials of the Department and representatives of the plastics and chemical firm EUREAC with whom subject had recently been involved, established the

17

background to subject's illness. Interviews with the subject himself revealed that he was suffering from very deep-rooted delusions concerning what had occurred in the previous few days —for a time he had been working on the kidnap of Wolfgang Herm, the Vice-President of EUREAC, though latterly Secretary Prinz had taken him off the case at the onset of the symptoms described above.

"Taking all these factors into account I was able to make a confident diagnosis of paranoid schizophrenia and I proceeded to treat subject accordingly. A course of chorpromazine is indicated in these circumstances and this was initiated. However, subject notably failed to respond. The dose was increased and towards the end of May subject began to exhibit mild symptoms of incipient Parkinsonism and biperiden was accordingly prescribed.

"By 6 June the violent aggressive symptoms had almost entirely disappeared. However, in apparently rational conversation subject continued to insist, in face of all the evidence to the contrary, that he had been on the point of being murdered by the company secretary of EUREAC and had been saved only at the last moment by the intervention of Baron de Merle, the company's president. No amount of rational persuasion could shift these absurd delusions nor the extremely paranoid fear that he was still at risk. He kept insisting (and thus exhibited an absolutely classic symptom of his illness) that he 'knew too much', that it was unthinkable that 'he would be allowed to live' once he was discharged from the hospital.

"By now subject was physically in good health, though still prone to extended depressions. Taking all this into consideration, and after consultation with my colleagues, I ordered a short course of electro-convulsive therapy to be administered under anaesthetic, and without subject's knowledge.

"Subject's response to this, by the third instalment of said treatment, was extremely gratifying, and after the fifth it was decided to bring the treatment to a close. Subject however continued to suffer from depression and when he suggested that he transfer for a period of convalescence to Heart's Haven, a private psychiatric home run by Doctor Liszt, I welcomed the move.

"Since then (5 July) I have had four extended interviews with subject and I can now confidently report that he has made a remarkable recovery. No doubt this has been very considerably promoted by subject's own personality which, in health, appears to be very positive, capable of great self-control and supported by deep-rooted beliefs in such 'virtues' as restraint, loyalty, hard work, 'doing one's duty', and so on. In fact I think it probable, though I must now add that I am writing speculatively, that his initial illness arose from a conflict between these inner dynamics and outer tension, particularly relating to his wife who has been ill for some time, and about whom he undoubtedly has deep-rooted feelings of guilt.

"It is too early to say yet whether subject should be returned to his onerous duties as Commissioner for Public Order, involving as these do a very considerable burden of responsibility. However, I doubt if continued clinical treatment is indicated either. On the whole, though with reservations, I accept that the assignment in the Virtue Islands as Internal Security Adviser to IBOBRAS may well be a suitable stepping stone to fully restored health."

Secretary Prinz nodded wisely, appended a cryptic squiggle of his pencil beneath the doctor's signature, and glanced over the three typewritten sheets that came next. As he did, his eyebrows came together in a frown and absently he began to restuff his still-hot pipe bowl with tobacco. Presently the clouds of smoke began to swirl again about his noble head.

"From Doctor Liszt, Heart's Haven Clinic, Province of Brabt, 22 August 1980.

"I have been asked for my opinion as to the health of Commissioner Argand. First let me say that I believe both the diagnosis and prognosis of my colleague Doctor Rebb of the Brabt State Hospital were mistaken. Commissioner Argand, though already on the road to recovery, was indeed mentally ill when he came into my care, but not from paranoid schizophrenia. In my considered estimation he had suffered a perfectly understandable breakdown consequent on severe blows to what had hitherto been his accepted and unquestioned view of the society in which we live. Commissioner Argand has been known to me for some five years during which I have been treating his wife. During that time I have come to appreciate that his is indeed a highly complex nature: on the one side he is intelligent, receptive, capable of realistically sound judgments, even of penetrating insight. On the other he is extremely rigid in his basic approach to life, adhering through thick and thin to certain outmoded principles and beliefs including a blind faith in the social order we live under and the hierarchies that apparently maintain it, coupled with extreme conservatism of outlook . . . ."

Secretary Prinz's eyebrows rose further. Dr Liszt was of course a radical. There was a file on him, a fairly fat one, and more than once his orthodox colleagues had asked for an enquiry into his methods. In short he was a potential trouble-maker. However . . . Prinz sucked on his pipe and read on.

"The combination is of course, from a clinical point of view, a dangerous one and is, at the very least, likely to keep the patient under considerable and continuous strain. When the stress becomes too much he is likely to retreat not into schizophrenia but

20

depression, and this I think is what happened to Commissioner Argand following his involvement in the Herm Affair. I have treated him accordingly and he has made a very speedy recovery, pulling back to something like his old level of apparent stability. On the whole I feel I can recommend his temporary appointment to a post with a purely advisory function as a stepping stone to reassuming fuller responsibilities.''

Which, thought Prinz, though not entirely satisfactory, will do. It will cover me. EUREAC, or rather elements in EUREAC, want Argand out of the Province, at least until they feel more sure of him than they do now. That is understandable. IBOBRAS will accept Argand's temporary appointment as advisor on internal security, and indeed will pay him nearly twice the salary he is getting as Commissioner for Public Order . . . . It seems, thought Prinz, the best solution.

IBOBRAS was the Spanish-based construction firm which was to build the American Base on Santa Caridad, in the Spanish-held Virtue Islands off the west coast of Africa. It was virtually owned by EUROSTRUCT which shared directors, contracts and financial links with EUREAC, and Prinz was on the boards of all three corporations.

For a moment a hard cold edge of reality intruded into the Secretary's mind. It was the *only* solution. They'd kill Argand all right if they thought he was still a threat. Can't have that. He's a good chap. In the right areas a useful chap. It had been a mistake to involve him in the Herm/EUREAC business, best get him out while we can, see how he fares. Of course, if it seems he's going to continue to stir things up, well then . . .

This Sam Peters, thought Prinz, the American Liaison Officer between the Pentagon, the Spanish authorities and IBOBRAS, seems a sensible fellow. I'll ask him to keep an eye on Argand, make sure he's keeping his nose out of the wrong corners.

At all events, sending Argand to Santa Caridad would postpone a difficult decision for a month or so, and he reached for his phone. Secretary Prinz owed his position, at least in part, to his readiness to postpone awkward decisions.

III

THE second stage of the flight to Benítez Airport, Santa Caridad, was far more tolerable than the first — even, at times, pleasant. After a four-hour delay at Barajas during which the more susceptible of the passengers were treated for shock and all but the hand luggage was searched yet again, they had been put back on to the plane, or another exactly the same. The difference was that, with the departure of the oil sheikh, those who were able to pay were invited to travel first class.

The bomb had hurt none of them — it had exploded in the unloading bays at the other end of the conveyor, killing a luggage handler and maiming two more. Some said it had been a Basque device, others that the sheikh had indeed been the target. Argand kept his suspicions to himself; however, he, like the others, had had a fright and so had felt able to take a proper dose of the pills prescribed by Doctors Liszt and Rebb. Normally he ignored them, distrusting the chemical euphoria they induced and fearing that he might come to rely on them.

He had a good view now, and enjoyed his first sight of Africa — the north-west tip laid out like a relief map with the Rif Mountains nodding across the Straits of Gibraltar to the Sierra Nevada dipping into the evening haze behind. The food was almost edible, and he had a companion who was entirely unexceptionable; a Professor Shiner, who had silver hair, half-moon glasses, rosy cheeks, and who worked away at some papers and books until Argand spoke to him. Then he seemed happy to chat while the stewardess served them with Tío Pepe and scotch.

"This Benítez," Argand asked, indicating Shiner's books, "is he anything to do with Benítez airport?"

"Jorge Benítez. Indeed he is." The Professor smiled cherubically. "Las Guavas' favourite son, and, not to put too fine a point on it, my bread and butter." His accent was Edinburgh educated, a more pleasant way of speaking English than most.

"What did he do?" Argand was almost sure there had been no mention in the folders and brochures provided by IBOBRAS.

"He wrote a good deal of books. Plays as well, but mostly novels. The Spanish language's answer to Scott, Balzac and Dickens. If he hadn't existed Hispanic pride would have invented him." The Professor twinkled. "Perhaps it did. At all events a big effort to reinvent him is certainly under way."

This was lost on Argand, though he suspected some sort of academic joke. The Professor talked on, talking was his forte. "Our Jorge. He was born in Las Guavas, left when he was nineteen, returned only twice, obviously hated the place. But he was tactful enough to say that the considerable boat journey was intolerable. *Mal de mer.* So he spent most of his life in Madrid when he wasn't swanning around London and Paris. Sea-sickness didn't stop him crossing the Channel, or even the Bay of Biscay. Still, apart from the odd general and admiral, Falangists for the most part, he's about all the Islands have in that line so they make a fuss of him. A considerable fuss."

He prodded the papers and a blue plastic folder inscribed *IV Congreso Internacional Beníteziano.*

"They do us very well. About a hundred of us. We meet and talk and talk and talk and they put us in good hotels, or the university residence which used to be a hotel but went bankrupt. In return we tell them what a marvellous writer the old man was, a sound chap as well, and on our say-so they print huge editions for the schools and make a fortune selling them on the mainland. It's a good racket and entirely harmless. Beneficial to everyone, not least the school-kids who might otherwise be occupied with homosexuals like Lorca or Communists like Alberti and Machado."

None of this really interested the Commissioner, but nor did it jar the temporary euphoria.

"What sort of things do you find to say about this man?" he asked.

The Professor laughed, and then sipped his sherry. "Well, there's no shortage of topics, believe me. My own particular line at the moment is the colour red in the early novels. Since these deal almost entirely with wars both civil and international, it's a colour that gets mentioned often. I can go on for *hours* about *El color rojo en las primeras novelas de Jorge Benítez.*" His Spanish was accented in exactly the same way as his English. A listener unfamiliar with both tongues would not have heard the difference. "However, the best gardens have their serpents and that of Academe is no exception." He prodded what was obviously a programme for the Congress. " 'Towards a Structuralist Approach to Jorge Benítez', a Frenchman's contribution, of course. I shall give that one a miss. And here's another. Dr Françoise Brunot on '*Las Dos Naciones* — An Unstable Text'. Sounds harmless enough, but beneath those innocent words lies the Marxist approach, I fear. Especially as she has picked a novel which is to some extent about class. Ah well. She's not unattractive and I shall enjoy breaking the odd lance with her. The only trouble is these people take themselves so seriously. And they are quarrelsome. It's a bad omen, I think, that this is to be the *Fourth* International. . . ."

He chatted on, unaware that the name Françoise Brunot had triggered Argand's memory, and that the policeman had had momentary but total recall of a confrontation that had taken place twelve years earlier. He had been interrogating a girl student, as

25

he was bound to do under the rules of the emergency, about her affiliations, and she, bleeding from a scalp wound, had refused to answer, had instead insisted that he record that she was making an official complaint of police brutality. It was a bitter memory, troubled by his awareness of the girl's apparent wholesomeness, of her anger, of his own utter hate of everything represented by the ideas she held, of the causes she had been demonstrating for. The same girl, woman now, had been on the plane, in the transit hall, was presumably still somewhere nearby, in the tourist section behind him. Argand shuddered at the thought, but could not be sure why.

"And tell me, sir, what brings *you* to the Virtue Islands?"

Argand pulled himself together and told the academic that he was a policeman, that he had been seconded to advise on security at the American Base.

Shiner knew of it, had heard that there was opposition to it on the islands.

"Can't think why," he went on. "Bound to bring money in and they need that. Money and employment now the tourist boom is fading. Hard times round the corner — this Base will be just the thing, especially for the construction industry. I suppose San Salvador SA will be handling it."

Argand frowned. "I think not. A firm called IBOBRAS has the overall contract."

"IBOBRAS? Mainland concern. That won't please the islanders. But I suppose it's too big a job for them to handle on their own."

"You seem to know Santa Caridad very well."

Shiner agreed that he did, explained that thirty years earlier he had written his doctoral thesis on Jorge Benítez and had been coming back at least once every three years ever since. He gossiped on and Argand was happy to let him. Apparently the big man on the island, "the uncrowned king", was Salvador Guzmán who owned the firm San Salvador SA and was a friend, of sorts, of

Shiner: Guzmán apparently saw himself as a latter day Mycenas, had put up money for the Benítez Congress, and patronized the arts in other ways too. He was even thought to be something of a separatist.

"I thought they were all left wing?" Argand interposed.

"Well, yes, the ones that get the headlines are. But really those are very unpopular — Marxist terrorists, you know, operating out of the African mainland. Nobody likes them, nobody wants them, and nobody takes seriously their claim that Las Virtudes are geographically part of Africa, not Europe. But many of the more solid citizens too would be happy to get away from Spain — if it could be made economically viable, that is."

The plane gently tipped the horizon into their sight and for a moment both men watched it, and the dark ocean beneath. The sun had already gone from the water though it still filled the cabin with a golden glow. The waves looked chill, ominous, empty.

"Sometimes you see whales, you know," said Shiner. "But not today. Not long now."

"The original inhabitants were African, I think," said Argand. "Yes?"

"IBOBRAS issued me with folders, brochures and so on, as well as plans of the Base. I think they said the natives were of African origin." He reached for his document case which was on the floor beside his seat, and put it on the table.

"Odd," said Shiner. "Your case is exactly the same as mine. *Pandore SA, Belge.* Mine was a handout, a perk. They've given them to all the major speakers at the Congress."

"Well, this was a perk too," said Argand. "From IBOBRAS, or anyway the parent company EUROSTRUCT."

"I suspect it's not really a coincidence. In fact, now you mention it, I believe I do recall that IBOBRAS are one of our sponsors this year."

Argand, still determined to demonstrate that the original

27

inhabitants of the Virtues were African, selected a small key on his keyring, and inserted it into the lock on the case. It would not budge. He tried the other lock. Again nothing. A cold sweat broke out on his forehead. It was dawning on him that this was not his document case after all. His had had a scratch on the left corner, his had opened with this key, his had surely been lighter . . .

Shiner, unaware of anything untoward, chatted brightly on. "African or not, there's no trace of them now. The Spaniards landed in 1475. By 1600 the native population had either been absorbed, hispanized, or exterminated. It depends on the colour of your history . . ."

The temptation to paranoia is difficult to resist; the temptation to write off rational if inconvenient fears as paranoia is as great and far more dangerous. Argand did not know why his case had been swapped for another, had no real reason to suppose that this new case might contain a second bomb, a bomb that might be triggered by lifting the lid.

"Ah. There goes the seat belt signal. Odd thing about this landing is that you never see the island until touchdown. The approach is entirely over water. At this point I always hope that the pilot knows his left from his right."

Muzak — again the syncopated Schubert. Argand realized that the Professor was nervous. Many people are at take-off and touchdown. The sea was now very close indeed — big, black, foam-flecked rollers running, it seemed, no more than a house height below them.

"You see, there are two runways. Side by side. Only a few yards apart. The first one developed cracks, crumbled up. Bad concrete. Cost poor old Guzmán a packet, it was his contract, you see. . . . If the pilot picks the wrong one, and it's been known to happen I believe, we're in for a bumpy time."

Argand sighted deeply, cleared his throat, and called for the stewardess — just as the wheels touched and rumbled, smoothly enough after all.

José Pérez, the chief of Las Guavas police and the man with whom Argand would be working most closely, was at Benítez Airport to meet him. It was natural he should take charge. Following his instructions, radioed from the control tower, the 707 was again evacuated with exemplary speed, Argand remaining till last of the passengers, and standing almost protectively over the suspect case. He watched them file through the first-class section towards the emergency exit, and noted amongst them the Indian who had sat next to him as far as Madrid, and then Françoise Brunot. Yes, he was sure it was the same girl, the girl from '68. Well, she at any rate had no reason to wish him well . . . though presumably she was not still suicidal.

At last all were off, including Argand. The plane was towed to a far corner of the field and bomb disposal men went aboard. It did not take them long to get the case open and though the contents were lethal enough, they did not explode. They were: six half-kilo bags of very high-quality heroin and a glossy magazine with an almost nude red-head on the cover.

IV

LYING on his back, head propped on pillows, Argand restlessly churned over the events of a day that had been far too full of incident for someone still convalescing from mental illness. Outside the Atlantic wind rattled the palm leaves and sent the lights from the road beyond rippling across his ceiling; behind the noise of the traffic he could hear the ocean — but none of this soothed, little of it was even noticed.

The point was — but for his wariness with a lock that would not budge as readily as he had expected, he could by now have been in a Santa Caridad jail charged with illegal possession of heroin, instead of relatively comfortable if sleepless in the Hotel Santa Teresa. This was not fanciful. Indeed it was not. He could see the pattern, play over in his mind the unfolding story that had not after all taken place.

The case would have been opened by customs officers and Argand identified. But then the telex messages would have tapped back and forth, perhaps an officer would have flown out from Brabt, an officer well briefed and disposed against Commissioner Argand. There were several who would fit that bill. Thirty years of scrupulously honest and conscientious police work was a sure way of making implacable enemies amongst one's colleagues. And a picture would have emerged — of a senior officer who had recently bungled an important job, who had been mentally ill, who had been shunted away into an advisory role, which was no doubt a prelude to an enforced early retirement.

And it would have been shown that Argand had access to heroin — had not a ring operating from an American NATO base not twenty miles from Brabt been busted only a week ago? And then Las Guavas is a free port, a trading post for almost every commodity in the world whose movement is restricted by tariffs, controls, laws — from arms to whisky, from gems to drugs. What better place to bring heroin for a quick sale; what place with better facilities for transferring the proceeds to some safe niche back in Europe? No doubt the Commissioner was planning a well-cushioned old age. . . .

Argand twisted away from this line of thought. It was a fruitless one — the plot had failed, Argand had not been arrested, far from it. Of course, once the heroin had been discovered, Pérez had questioned him closely but amicably enough — they were of a rank and it would not have done to start several weeks of collaboration as interrogator and suspect. Together they had quickly established a reasonable hypothesis as to when the cases had been exchanged. Clearly it had happened in the seconds before or after the explosion at Barajas Airport, Madrid. Argand was almost certain he had let his case go in the confusion, and felt too that a moment before someone had been pulling at it, trying to make him release it. The Indian had been near him, the Indian who had sat next to him, and Françoise Brunot too. Also the Englishman who had started the panic. The Indian had earlier offered Argand a magazine similar to the one found in the case, he really was the most likely. . . .

And there Pérez, a large man with crinkly grey hair and a large nose, who wore a rather smart pale ochre suit, had, Argand considered, got it wrong. The Indian, who was actually of mixed Pakistani and English parentage, born in Gibraltar, was known to him. Salim Tumbal Robertson was his name and he worked as courier for his stepfather, a gem dealer called Joachim Joachim. A gem dealer who had switched to drugs? But Pérez had been quite happy to assume that the cases had been swapped by accident and he was confident that they would pick Salim up soon, but less confident that they would be able to make a charge stick — the evidence against him was now slim, barely more than Argand's recollection of a magazine whose cover he had been at pains to ignore anyway.

None of which would really do. Argand got off the bed and padded across to the wash-basin where he rinsed his face and drank a glass of water; then he snapped on the light and looked around him, momentarily distracted again by his surroundings: the bland vulgarity and pointless luxury annoyed him. He felt that the colour TV, the radio, the air-conditioning, the third tap marked in four languages "ice-cold drinking water" represented a sybaritism gone mad; that the satin covers, the deep carpet, the silk wall-covering added up to a room more suited to a whore than a policeman. He was feeling dyspeptic too. The wienerschnitzel supplied by the hotel after Pérez had finally dropped him off at nearly midnight had been dry, perhaps a cold one warmed through. Away from the mainly potato-based peasant dishes of Brabt, Argand almost invariably ate wienerschnitzel.

Next to the sedatives ignored on his dressing-table, and the wood-backed brushes he had owned for thirty years, were the soda mints he always took with him. He took two, put them under his tongue, put out the light again and stood in the window. There for a time he watched a light mechanically flashing on the end of an island that lay like a whale on the horizon, and the thoughts churned on.

No. It would not do. Even given the fact that at least three people on the plane had had identical document cases (*Pandore SA, Belge*) — thanks to the generosity of EUROSTRUCT and IBOBRAS — it was still unthinkable that the heroin had arrived in

32

his possession by accident. Coincidences happen, but only in the minds of defence lawyers pleading against circumstantial evidence — policemen ignore them, work always on the assumption that they do not occur.

Argand became conscious of anguish. His mind was twisting and turning like a rabbit in a trap, like the towel that had appeared — he could not remember how — in his hands and which he was strangling as if it were a venomous snake. For five months doctors, family, colleagues, superiors had conspired to make him believe a lie. Moreover common sense and survival instinct had insisted that it would be better for him if he did. They had used a barrage of drugs, and ECT involuntarily administered without his knowledge. A fellow patient had told him as much. Yet he knew, and the knowledge would remain with him until he died, no matter what they did to remove it, that they had been about to kill him, had reprieved him only for reasons of expediency.

He had to face up to the fact that if they wanted him dead five months ago they might well want him in a Spanish jail for the rest of his life: it was as good a way of rendering him harmless as any. The question was — what was he, now, going to do about it? For a moment he felt wretchedly weak, insecure, lost, as near to despair — which he called self-pity — as he ever could be. What chance could there possibly be for him? What chance against the power of a multi-national like EUREAC backed by a corrupt administration? One way or another they would get him in the end. But this would not do. With a sudden, brisk gesture of determination he turned away from the window and almost stamped back to the unlikeable, alien bed. He would do what he could for as long as he could. He had the end of a thread in his hands — this Salim Robertson and Joachim Joachim — other clues would come. He would follow them back, inch by inch, to the originators of this plot against him, and then, if he got far enough to be sure

33

exactly where his enemies lay, he would see what could be done about them.

Nothing to be done now, except sleep. Pérez was coming for him at eleven o'clock in the morning. He would have time to make a start before then.

Towards dawn, and unaided by any medication other than soda mint, Commissioner Jan Argand briefly slept, his dreams untroubled by his fears — real or imagined.

At the desk in the morning the clerk handed Argand a card. The heading was printed with the insignia and address of LADI, the airline to the islands. Beneath, typed with an IBM typewriter, he read: "*Señor*, a document case which we believe is yours has been handed in at the above address. We would be grateful if you would identify and collect it at your earliest convenience. Assuring you always of our most obliging attentions, LADI.'

The address was in the Calle Mayor de Triana, the desk clerk said it was a short taxi drive away, that yes there was a bank there, several in fact, and the Post Office too.

The Calle Mayor turned out to be a pedestrian precinct — what had once been the carriageway was now paved and dotted with stone seats. There was too a rather strange series of paintings on large metal sheets set at intervals on two-metre posts down the whole length of the street. The first impression was one of colour, liveliness, but almost all were modernistic in one way or another, and in several the paint had been applied mechanically with sprays or rollers. To Argand they represented an appalling collapse of taste and skill.

Still the air was warm and bright, the area cheerful with the first busy-ness of morning. Sunburnt tourists, slovenly in raffia sun-hats, shorts and flip-flops, contrasted with the locals —

white-shirted or suited, the older women in black, the younger always smart — who serviced the shops and offices. The shops were extraordinary, reflected the status of Las Guavas as a free port — treasure houses filled with the most up-to-date luxury goods: SLRs, miniatures, lenses, all the paraphernalia the well-heeled photographer likes to buy; music centres, video chains including colour cameras; furs, leather goods and, above all, gem shops, filled with precious and semi-precious stones glowing or glittering in chunky modern settings of gold or platinum.

Soon he came to what looked like the principal branch of the Banco de Santa Caridad, a marble-faced edifice with bronze window frames and bronze pillars flanking a wide doorway. It was guarded by two military police, smart in khaki drill, white helmets, white gloves, armed with machine carbines. Inside, Argand joined a queue of five or six foreigners at the *cambio* desk, and looked around him with a professional eye. Although the large hall was pleasantly old-fashioned with marble everywhere and bronze fittings to match, it had most of the modern safety devices. In the centre of the vaulted roof a spherical camera, mounted like a mine with protruding lenses, slowly revolved. The four-boothed caisse, *caja* was the Spanish word, was well-protected with bullet-proof glass and electronically controlled catches. Behind it Argand could see the doors to the vaults. These too were modern, steel lined and fitted with locks like steering wheels. He signed his cheques, was given a coloured slip with a number, and joined the queue at the *caja*.

At this point there was a slight commotion. One of the military policemen came down the hall, and behind him marched two blue-uniformed security guards. They had Perspex visors over their faces, heavy revolvers and truncheons swung at their belts. Between them they pulled a low steel trolley. A third remained at the doors, and no doubt there were more outside. Passes were posted through a slit on the reinforced glass, an official — he looked very senior, in an immaculate slate-blue suit and knitted black silk tie — checked these electronically and authorized the opening of the outer doors. As he turned towards the vaults, Argand noticed that he had a clover-leaf mark below his right ear. He now span the wheels, stood back, and one of the cashiers moved forward to drag open the heavy doors. The trolley was pushed nearer, one of the guards took up a position near the glass door that connected the *caja* to the main hall, the other watched as the trolley was loaded with blue bags, some chunky with specie, the others square with stacked notes. Receipts were exchanged, scrutinized, signed, and then the whole process unwound itself until at last everything was back as it had been, the vaults locked, the glass door closed, the manager back in his office, and the police on the doorstep. Argand's number was called, and he was paid his pesetas.

It had been done efficiently, he thought, according to the book, perhaps too much so. His professional eye had detected signs that the ritual had become routine, as though its meaning was half forgotten.

He walked on past more gem shops, and a sports goods shop filled with golf clubs, scuba diving gear, and steel tennis rackets. Next door there was a large café. People were sitting outside, and Argand thought he might return there for a coffee. Four soldiers sat on the edge of the flow of passers-by. They were arguing insolently with the waiter, a harassed man carrying a tray laden with chocolate, *churros*, and coffees. Argand paused, seeing an incident in the offing, but two policemen in blue uniforms were on the corner, watching the progress of the row.

The waiter raised his voice, swung his tray slightly behind him so he could lean past one of the soldiers. He stabbed at the bill with his finger, and repeated what he had been saying more loudly. As he did so one of the other soldiers, a tall, red-faced blond, reached round him and nudged the tray off balance — cups, plates, everything tumbled to the paving with an extended crash. The four soldiers bayed with laughter as the waiter grovelled at their feet. The two policemen looked on — stone-faced, perhaps even angry, but motionless.

Argand felt angry too, but with the language difficulty there was nothing he could do. He noted that the soldiers wore forage caps with little tassles and had death's head flashes on their upper arms.

At the LADI offices everything was done smoothly. His case was brought out, he examined it — *Pandore SA, Belge* — and opened it.

Everything was there — handouts about Santa Caridad and Las Guavas, plans of the Base, PR stuff about its role in the defence of the West. The only thing was that the order of it all had been reversed. What had been on top was now on the bottom, and vice versa, all through. Someone had been through the lot, examining each piece of paper in turn.

"It's all here," he said at last. "But, forgive me asking, has anyone here opened this since it was brought in?"

They were horrified at the thought. A cursory glance had been enough to assure them that it belonged to someone employed by IBOBRAS and connected with the Base. IBOBRAS had confirmed that Commissioner Argand had been on the flight from Amsterdam and was staying at the Hotel Santa Teresa. After that the case had stayed in the safe until the Commissioner himself walked in.

With skin pricking, palms suddenly moist but voice level, Argand asked if they knew who had brought it back. Yes, they knew. Dr Françoise Brunot. She was staying at the university residence about ten kilometres out of town, but attending the

37

Congreso Beníteziano which was being held in the Casa de Colón, in the old town. All this they had had to find out, in case the case had not after all been collected. She had brought it in this morning, had in fact been waiting at the door when they opened, on her way to the Casa de Colón.

At the Post Office Argand telexed his request for information on Salim Robertson and Joachim Joachim to CRIC in Brussels, the computerized criminal filing centre for the whole of Europe. Then, using the code for political files this time, he added the name of Brunot. Coincidences do not occur in a policeman's life, and he felt now that he would like to know the latest about her too.

V

CONSIDERING he was meant to be in poor mental health Argand retained a remarkable ability to push an anxiety out of his mind once he had done everything he could about it — for the time being. Moreover he was a conscientious man, professionalism was a matter of pride with him: throughout most of the rest of the day he gave almost all his attention to his role as Internal Security Adviser to IBOBRAS.

Already he rather liked Pérez, who was waiting for him on his return: the island police chief was a large, dour, even melancholy man, clearly conscious of the authority of his position and presumably of its responsibilities too. There was no nonsense about him, except possibly in the splendour of his clothes which were superbly cut from fine materials, and the care that had been lavished on his hair, nails, skin even. But there was nothing of the dandy in the man's manner and the Protestant Brabanter put down these extravagances not to vanity but southern *mores* — and in this he was not far wrong. Spaniards expect the powerful and rich to look powerful and rich. Moreover a police chief of Pérez's standing is expected to be rich as well as powerful — he would be suspected of incompetence if he were not.

But standing with Pérez in the foyer of the Santa Teresa — which had more character than its rooms, being done out with palms in pots, wicker-work furniture and original art nouveau décor — was Sam Peters, to whom Argand immediately took a dislike.

The American Liaison Officer was fat, with grey, close-cropped hair, glasses, and a walrus moustache which usually harboured crumbs. His suit, a crumpled lightweight, did not fit and showed damp patches beneath the arms. He shook hands moistly and bonhomously, yet his eyes behind his glasses remained characteristically expressionless.

"Why hallo there, Commissioner — come aboard. This is a rare privilege, you know that José? The Commissioner here has the reputation of being the greatest IS man this side of the water. You know what, Jan — it's a great relief to me that José let you off that heroin smuggling rap — you'd have been no use to us in the can," and he punched Argand playfully on the arm. Argand flinched. He suspected Peters might make heroin smuggling a running joke — and he was right.

The site lay to the east of Las Guavas along the north coast of the island, but Pérez suggested they should take a detour, give Argand a chance to get the feel of the whole place. They travelled in a large black Mercedes which Pérez drove with accomplished care. More than once Argand felt the Spaniard was recognized — by traffic policemen naturally enough, but once or twice by similarly dressed men in similarly grand cars. A finger raised from a steering wheel, a head tipped in the slightest of nods — clearly José Pérez was someone to be reckoned with in Las Guavas.

Argand had not so far been impressed with the city and what he saw now did little to alter his first judgement. A well engineered clearway followed the curve of a bay past parks and hotels with clubs, beaches and marinas between it and the ocean, yet there was a shabby air to almost everything — boarded-up sites awaiting development alternated with blocks where the concrete was already streaked, the paint flaked, and the sidewalks had never been made up. At the end was the port, a recent construction with hoists for containers, warehouses, and large freighters in the roads. Beneath a low parched hill there was an oil refinery with a tanker standing off.

At the port gates the Mercedes turned inland down a wide boulevard that did have some style, grandeur even, though it was entirely modern. Argand noticed that it was called Avenida de Venezuela. This took them directly across an isthmus perhaps two kilometres wide and so on to another coast road much like the first — again a bay curved to another headland about five kilometres away, but with a sweep that had been lacking before. In the middle a wide valley opened into an estuary protected by a mole. Between the hills behind Argand caught a glimpse of San Cristóbal, the extinct volcano in the middle of the island. The old city of Las Guavas was clustered round the estuary, dominated by the twin spires of a small cathedral. A little later they passed a shabby but large theatre, right on the sea front. It was no surprise to see that it was called the *Teatro Benítez*.

The road, now virtually a motorway, swept inconsiderately on through villages of tiny huts which huddled wherever shingle allowed fishing boats to be beached. Slogans had been sprayed on every wall large enough to take them, on the occasional bridges, even on the road surface itself. The most common of these was simply '*No a la Base*', stencilled and repeated again and again. Sometimes it was accompanied by a crude rendering of a nuclear mushroom cloud.

"Is there much opposition to the Base?" Argand asked.

Pérez twisted uncomfortably in the leather upholstery, caught between the official line which was to minimize or deny any such thing, and awareness that Argand should know the truth since he was there to advise on how it should be coped with.

Peters intervened. "Come on, José, there's opposition all right. But nothing we can't handle."

"Considerable opposition," Pérez said at last. "But not very important. Politically inspired, of course. We have high unemployment, many idle people with nothing better to do. But all people of any importance on the island are solidly for it."

"Have there been demonstrations?"

"Of course, and we are very well equipped to deal with them. I have five hundred full-time riot police and a thousand part-time reservists. We have the latest IS equipment too — sixteen Panhards, Armoured Personnel carriers with the T 20 turret and twenty GKN Sankey AT 105s, with ten more on order. The trouble is there always seem to be labour problems in England and they are behind on their delivery dates."

"I was at the first trials of the AT 105 in '77," said Argand. "It seemed an excellent vehicle, especially in the Rolls-Royce version. Are yours armed?"

"They sure ought to be armed," said Peters. "I've been doing all I can my end to get them armed. I shan't be happy IS-wise until I know old José's got some real fire-power under his belt."

Pérez's expression grew more melancholy than ever. "It's a controversial question here in Santa Caridad. As you know the Panhards can be fitted with a 20mm cannon or adapted to take an 81mm mortar. Now I wanted these but the military and Madrid ministry said no."

"Is there a military garrison on the island?"

"In effect two. There is a regiment of infantry with all the usual support groups barracked in the hills above Las Guavas. Then on the island of Santa Prudencia which you can see on the horizon there is a regiment of the Foreign Legion."

"So you don't really need cannon and mortars of your own."

"Well, I'm not so sure. The garrison are conscripts from industrial mainland towns. They are well organized where they come from and we know they have contacts with our labour force. I am not sure we could rely on them if it came to a fully armed

42

confrontation. And there are problems with the Legion. They are an élite fighting group who have seen active service in the Sahara. Now the war there is over, for Spain anyway, they are bored. They always cause trouble when they come into Las Guavas on furlough. If I had to use them I'd lose the support of the entire population, not just the people against the Base."

Argand remembered the bullies with tassles on their caps. Pérez agreed that they would indeed have been legionaries.

"Say, perhaps Jan here would back you with the Governor and Madrid, help you get that artillery — they ought to listen to him."

But Argand would not be drawn. He did not believe police should be armed beyond what was needed for riot control. As far as he was concerned, a situation which required cannon and mortar had ceased to be a civil matter.

Pérez drove on for a moment or two.

"You'll probably get a better idea of it all in two or three days' time. We're going to have a general strike on our hands and a mass demonstration."

"Why's that?"

Pérez looked grim. Peters pushed in, his voice suddenly high, almost jeering. "Sore point, eh José? What it is, Jan, is this. IBOBRAS are landing a giant earth digger, a real monster, which has to be got across town to the site. No one wants it, not island labour nor island capital, but it sure is going to save Uncle Sam a hell of a lot of money."

"I'd like you along, if it does come to a confrontation," Pérez added.

Argand was pleased. "Of course," he said.

The site when they reached it was much as Argand had expected it to be from the maps and plans he had seen. Over all it was shaped like a chemical retort — a bulb with a long narrow strip or neck

43

branching from the top of it. The round part, irregularly shaped, was about six kilometres in diameter and lay in one of the few relatively flat areas of the island. Behind it were hills, those to the south being particularly steep. To the north lay the ocean. The neck of the retort followed the north coast line in an easterly direction for about twenty-five kilometres and was at first quite wide. Later it narrowed to a narrow strip between steep and rocky hills and the sea. It was here that the giant earth digger would be used — to dig rocket silos and then a long snaky trench up and down which, beneath a concrete skin, Missile-X would be continuously and randomly trundled — a moving target no Russian rocket could be sure of hitting. All this would be sealed off with every security device known to man — proof, it was intended, against any interference less than direct hits with nuclear war heads. But the bowl or bulb was another matter, and this was Argand's main concern.

Pérez drove them up a slope to relatively high ground where they got out, and with the maps taken from his newly recovered case Argand followed while Peters described what would happen below them. The American spoke rapidly, enthusiastically, using structures and vocabulary that often left Argand — whose English had been learnt on an RAF station in East Anglia after the fall of Brabt in 1940 — struggling to understand.

The bowl would be vulnerable, both to demonstrations and terrorist infiltration. Here would be all the back-up and support systems the Base would need: administration blocks, servicing workshops, stores for everything from drinking water shipped from State-side to spare nuclear warheads; and also living facilities for the scientists and technicians who would run the Base and the military who would guard it. The specifications included a theatre, soft ball pitches, swimming pools, three restaurants, a marina, and parking on a one man one car basis. Peters wasn't too happy about this last — it might not, he thought, be enough.

What actually lay in front of them was a piece of hell.

Its recent past was still discernible — it had been a very fertile area, peasant farmed in small parcels and strips many of which had had dwelling places on them, sheds and barns. Tobacco, tomatoes, cotton, guavas, pineapple and sugar-cane had all grown in rich and varied profusion, the land often yielding three crops in a year. Now two tracks, each dead straight and each a hundred metres wide had been driven into the very centre of the area, meeting there to form a harsh right-angle. Ruin spread on either side of these — fields and orchards had been churned up, walls put down, irrigation channels fractured so crops withered in patches where they had been suddenly parched while water gathered in sullen stagnant pools at the feet of still turning wind pumps. Barns and shacks had been reduced to brittle heaps of splintered wood and cart tracks churned into axle-deep morasses. Huge trucks, all boldly labelled San Salvador SA, pitched and rolled across the *vega*, dumping loads of aggregate on the layer of top soil that half a millennium of careful farming had built up.

Yet for Argand, as for the others, the whole business appeared only as a complex of IS problems, and this conditioned the way he looked at everything he saw. Thus, groves of guava trees on the north-facing slopes of the hills overlooking the centre of the bulge, appeared to him as likely cover for rocket or mortar attack. It did not matter to him that guavas had grown there for four hundred years — the first this side of the Atlantic had been planted there. And a little later, when they had driven deeper into the site, a shanty town of two-room adobe huts clinging to tufa slopes which in places had been hollowed out to provide a third room, became simply an obstruction to what, in his IS theory, he called "a vent road". The map showed the small steep hills, but there was no indication that people lived there.

45

In answer to a query from Argand, Pérez consulted a surveyor working with a road gang. While they spoke in Spanish Argand watched small dark children playing in a dry ditch. They looked like gypsies, he thought. Four women with black shawls over their heads stared impassively at the Mercedes. One of them was actually spinning thread out of a bag of raw wool and winding it on to a weighted distaff. Perhaps not gypsies but American Indians. Had any been brought here from the Hispanic colonies? Argand didn't know.

"There will be no problem," Pérez said, as he got back in. "These are all squatters, they've no right to be here. You can have your road here."

The Mercedes moved on.

"Why 'vent' road?" asked Peters. "Why do you call it that?"

Argand explained. To disperse a mass demonstration with a minimum of fuss it was essential that the demonstrators had somewhere to go. There should be three vent roads at the point where they would be challenged by IS forces.

"The aim is to break the strength of the demonstration without breaking its cohesion. Each individual will become frightened if he thinks he can be isolated from the rest in the presence of the IS force, so he clings in self-defence to his companions. So you try to split the mob three ways rather than disperse it, syphon it off to neutral areas where it can disperse of its own volition. One thing one should never try to do is turn a mob round, make it go back the way it came."

"See what I mean," crowed Peters. "Is not this guy the greatest IS expert in history? Psychology, that's the name of the game, eh Jan? You have to be a real psychologist."

They drove on through the broken fields. Grey powder coated glossy foliage and fruit and the harsh grunt and roar of bulldozers, the monotonous scream of trucks grinding through churned-up dust in low gear made conversation all but impossible.

Once they had to wait while an earth-mover bearing the usual blazon crossed the track in front of them.

"Salvador Guzmán is my father-in-law," Pérez suddenly shouted above the racket. "He has sub-contracted the site clearance from IBOBRAS."

"But not the construction work, eh José? Too bad. You can't win them all."

Pérez looked more melancholy than ever and drove on. At last they left the bowl and the road began to climb into volcanic hills. The soil.was cinders and only bananas seemed now to be worth cultivating. Argand found them almost obscene with their phallic flowers, and bunches of fruit supported on crutches. Glimpses of San Cristóbal became more frequent. They could see silvery and white gleams from the spherical and rectangular structures perched on the rim of the extinct crater, and even the intricate metal lacework of the radio telescopes.

"Impressive, eh?" said Peters. Argand, thinking that he was being invited to admire a natural phenomenon, agreed. But Peters was referring to the SPADATS on the top.

"Space Detection and Tracking Systems," he explained. "That's really the heart of it all, that's where the really clever stuff is. You'd be surprised what they can do, the information they can collect and feed back to Illiac-4."

Argand's bristly eyebrows contracted. Peters interpreted what may have been a sign of boredom as one of puzzlement.

"That's the computer, back in Moffett. Series of linked computers, I should say — the biggest brain in the world. And it ties in with DARPA too. That's the Defence Advanced Research Projects Agency. They're working out the effects of storms, waves, even whales on the inputs we get from the sonars. By 1985 we'll be able to drop a nuke on the nose of every sub Charlie has

47

out there. Then we'll see who calls the tune. No more Afghanis-
tans then, eh?"

Although this was good news for Argand he could not suppress a
small yawn.

Peters commiserated: "Hell, you must still be whacked. I bet
you've no way recovered from your ordeal in Madrid. And then,
on top of everything, Joey here tried to bust you for dope-
smuggling. It wasn't kind, José, not kind at all."

It was the fourth time Peters had brought it up. Argand felt a
chill creep on him as he looked past the American's glasses at cold
dead eyes. Why was Peters so obsessed with the heroin? Why did
he keep getting at Argand about it? His anxieties, dread, surfaced
at last in his mind like a pike rising in a tranquil pool.

VI

"AND so my friends I came to my conclusion. What I offer you today is by no means intended to be definitive, or self-justifying. I have simply done the spadework, sifted out a particular strand in Benítez's creative processes. It's for others now to make what they can of it. I've no doubt there will be those who take my approach, go into it more deeply, and throw new and genuine light on the great *oeuvre* we are met here to honour and explicate. Less happily I am also aware that I may have indicated an approach for the amateur psychoanalysts amongst us as well." Obsequious laughter. Good. ". . . I also fear that I may have weakened our defences against the post-Saussurians here. Personally, I remain an unrepentant anti-semiot . . ." No laughter. The joke won't really do in Spanish perhaps, Shiner thought. He went on: "But they don't worry me, for no one understands them. And finally there are of course our friends on the Left. And it is to them particularly that I make my final point. Let them not think that they have a monopoly in the colour red, in the powerful poetic and rhetorical uses to which it may be put. It would be absurd to say that just because Benítez saw in red an expressive tool of great power that he was therefore a red. Absurd, but by no means the most absurd device that has been used by those who would enlist our great author in the ranks of those who support an ideology that would, I most earnestly assure you, have been absolute anathema to that great upholder of all that was best in the nineteenth-century tradition of liberalism of which we are still, thank God, the happy heirs and benefactors."

49

Professor Shiner sat down and beamed at the quite definite reaction this produced. First a vociferous and noisy acclamation with, he was pleased to note, the odd boo amongst the bravos. Then, as it died, an excited buzz of conversation. That's put the cat amongst the pigeons, he thought, that's going to flush them out, casting down the gauntlet, seeking the direct confrontation with the Marxists that should have come about at the last *Congreso* three years ago, no more pussy-footing now. Whoops, here we go. Françoise Brunot on her feet, I thought she would be the first, waving her papers like the damned soul she is.

Outside, at the foot of the plateresque stairs a stranger stood, grey-suited, hatted, slightly uncertain, wondering what all the noise and excitement were about. A porter challenged him. He couldn't speak Spanish. *Francés? Sí.* A boy, uniformed like a page, trotted away over ancient flags to find a Congress secretary who could speak French. The porter indicated a polished wood bench, made appropriate gestures; dutifully Argand sat on it and waited, looked round the pleasant oak-panelled foyer, out into a patio, a cloister really, where an enormous green parrot hung upside down from an ancient tree, screamed, rattled its chain, and then said: "*Hola, hola, hola.*" "*Hola,*" called the porter, "*qué tal?*" "*Muy bien, gracias,*" screamed the parrot, "*hola.*"

"... More than once in his stimulating talk Professor Shiner referred to the celebrated close of *Cádiz 1848*, particularly to the paragraphs describing the lurid sunset over the Atlantic and the promise of a new dawn. I don't need to remind Congress that this was written in June 1870, that at that very moment the Spanish Regional Federation of the International was adopting the statutes of the Jura Federation as drawn up by Bakunin, that Benítez himself . . ." The high but firm voice was drowned in more noise, foot-stamping, boos, cheers, whistles even. The President of the session banged away with his gavel, Shiner beamed like a Buddha from the dais, a local photographer fired off his flash again and again.

Downstairs a girl clacked over the flags. Argand stood up, they spoke quietly for a moment, she looked at her watch. The evening session of the Congress was due to end just about now, if he waited here he would be sure to see Dr Brunot coming down the stairs, he would be able to catch her then, yes, she would be free, there was a half-hour break before they went to a reception at the Town Hall.

"Señor Presidente, the easiest and crudest way of attacking an opponent in this sort of context is to ascribe untenable views to her and then point out their absurdity. I have not said, in spite of what the last speaker imagines, and most certainly I do not believe, that Benítez was a Communist or anarchist in 1870. However, what can be very easily established is that he was a progressive, that *Cádiz 1848* and its predecessors were written in praise of what was truly the progressive class of the first half of the century, and, and, this is the point, that by 1870 Benítez was coming to recognize that objectively that same class was now a reactionary force, more concerned to consolidate its class gains than push on with the reforms, indeed revolution, it had begun . . . ."

More jeers and cheers, then a mid-western professor rose to propose a vote of thanks to Professor Shiner, which he did at length, using the occasion to advertize the courses in Spanish Studies at his college, and listing the farm implement manufacturers that had endowed them. He was seconded by a Frenchman who was brisk to the point of rudeness, and at last after one

51

more brief salvo of applause they all spilled out into the corridors.

At first sight they were a motley lot — ranging from the grey and immaculate, as immaculate as diplomats, to the almost hippy, though the latter, it should be said, were all clean and well fed. Yet to Argand they all seemed very much of a piece — all completely absorbed in what they had in common, like the members of an exclusive sect, a sect whose esoteric rituals scarely touch the real world. At least, at this moment they seemed aware of nothing at all, not the quietly beautiful sixteenth-century interiors, nor the outsider waiting at the bottom of the stairs. Like starlings each contributed to the group by making a noise — it was not required that they should listen to each other, only that the noise should be maintained at a satisfyingly high level.

Françoise Brunot was near the front as they came down — she looked flushed, excited, absorbed. A young man in tailored denims was next to her, throwing his arms in the air, expostulating, complaining, praising — three or four similarly dressed young men and women mimicked his performance on either side. Argand moved through the front runners, put himself in her path.

She stopped, puzzled at this sudden obstacle, then her face cleared, almost as if she were coming out of a trance.

"I know you, don't I? You were on the plane yesterday. Of course. It must have been your case I took back to the LADI offices."

"Yes. Do you mind if I have a word or two with you about that? To thank you, of course, but . . ."

"You must be Commissioner Argand. The Honest Commissioner. I'm Brabanter too," she dropped easily into their dialect, but a shadow passed across her face as she added, "and we've met before. I don't suppose you remember . . . ."

"If you don't mind . . ." Argand cut her off promptly.

"No. I don't suppose I mind. It won't take long, will it?"

"A minute or two."

She took his elbow and moved him out of the flow of people and into the cloister. A small exhibition had been arranged around the outer walls — blow-ups mostly of Santa Caridad and Las Guavas a hundred years ago; Benítez as a podgy baby, and then an earnest adolescent peered out of sepia backgrounds. In the middle a little fountain dribbled down black stones and through bright green ferns. The parrot had his say: "*Hola, hola, hola, muy bien gracias.*"

"Well, what do you want to know? I must say I thought I had done my bit by going to the trouble to take your case back to the LADI offices."

"Yes, indeed you did. And again, thank you very much. But there was a lot more to the incident than you know of, and I really must try to clear up what happened. First, when did you discover that you had my case?"

"Not until the Indian called and asked for me at the residence."

"I'm sorry. I didn't know he had done that. That must have been late last night."

"Yes, quite late. About half-past nine, I think. We were met here, you see, and a mini-bus had been laid on to take us up. Well, there was a certain amount of checking in to be done, and so I suppose it must have been half-past nine when I got to my room. I started to unpack, my clothes first, then I was just going to open the document case when there was a knock at the door and there was the Indian. He said that he had discovered that he had my case, and he believed I had his. He opened the one he had brought, and sure enough it had my books in it, papers and so on. I was very relieved. If I had lost that lot I should have been sunk — apart from anything else I should have lost the first draft of the paper I am to give the Congress at the end of the week, and the only other copy is back in Brabt."

"Then what happened?"

"Well, he got the case open and discovered it wasn't his after all. He was very distraught, very upset indeed. Literally he stood there wringing his hands. He kept saying something in English over and over again, I'm not sure what, my English isn't all that good, but the word 'Madrid' came into it, and then he went. Just like that. It was as if he had made up his mind about something and that was it."

"He didn't go through my case."

"Not really. Just enough to see it wasn't his. Perhaps to be sure it was yours."

"What did you do then? After he had gone?"

"I looked through it. Your case."

"Why?"

"Why not?"

They had reached the far end of the cloister. In front of them was a reproduction of a painting of four men in frock coats facing a firing squad. Las Guavas, 1832. Then Brunot's words sank in and a hysterical sort of anger began to swell inside him.

"Why not? Because it was not your case, you already knew it was not your case, why then should you look in it?" He paused, looked across the small courtyard. On the far side, above the green growth and the fountain, he could just make out Professor Shiner's face peering back at them over his half-moon glasses. He wondered: why is *he* taking an interest now? What's it got to do with *him*? He turned back to Brunot. "Who told you to look in my case?"

She stepped back. "What do you mean — who told me? No one told me. I was curious, that's all, just curious."

"Just curious?"

"That's right. I have an enquiring mind. It's something scholars are meant to have."

Argand clenched his hands in his jacket pockets. "So. I wonder what your enquiring mind made of the contents?"

She set her feet apart, her hands on her hips. "I discovered that the owner of the case was somehow connected with this awful Base the Americans are building on the north coast. And when I discovered that, my reaction was that I should put the whole lot on the fire. Now I wish I had."

"But you didn't. What did you do?"

"Nothing. I bundled the lot back into the case, and when I came down here first thing this morning I handed it in at the airline. You know that's what I did."

This time she did hesitate, perhaps failed to meet his gaze so directly. Nevertheless she repeated: "That's all. What else do you imagine I did with it? I can tell you I was glad to be rid of it. To me it was filth. I should have been happier if it had been filled with pornography or drugs."

A girl with red hair and no clothes. Six bags filled with heroin. She *was* in it. She was against him. Clearly nothing would be gained by continuing like this — he would have to find some other way of getting her to talk.

Brunot flinched away from a face suddenly white and gaunt, filled with hatred. The intensity in this man who had confronted her once before, many years before, and treated her then like a cipher, like an object to be processed and passed on, wounded though she had been, quite shocked her. The Honest Commissioner had a reputation for being cold, unemotional as well as honest — and indeed, at the enquiry following the student demonstration she had been leading when she was clubbed down, he had given clear and unequivocal evidence. The result was that the officer in charge of the riot police was disciplined. Well, all that was in the past. She felt pretty sure that the man in front of her now was almost out of his mind with anger.

They had completed the circuit of the cloister. Brunot looked up, saw the young man in denims waiting for her. He was carrying her document case, the one the Indian had brought to her room. She took it from him, propped it on her knee against the wall, riffled through the papers in it.

"Here, Commissioner. Take this. I am afraid it's in Spanish but

55

I'm sure sure you'll find someone to translate it for you."

He looked down at the duplicated sheets. Beneath a smudgy picture of an atomic explosion he read *Junta Popular Contra la Base*. At the foot of the first page was another picture — this time of serried ranks of rocket missiles.

"It'll give you some idea of just what sort of obscenity it is you're involved in here," she added.

Still white-faced he crumpled it up, hurled it away from him, and pushed his way out, shouldering to one side the twittering academics who were in his way.

"What's on tomorrow?" a voice behind him asked.

And the answer came: "Towards the Definition of Structural Parameters in the Early Works."

"*Hola*," screamed the parrot. "*Hola, hola, hola.*"

VII

AS he left the Casa de Colón Argand was preoccupied with the strength and ambiguity of his feelings about Brunot. For all her academic style, her plain denim dress with flap pockets over breasts, Françoise was an attractive woman. Indeed, in Argand's eyes the ordinary decency of her appearance was an advantage rather than otherwise. And she had spirit, a frank, open face with bright brown eyes, a body that was sturdy though small . . . and she was a professed Marxist. More recollections had come back to him — she had, he believed, organized a student and teacher strike at the university three years ago when the Dean of the Department of Social Engineering had refused to ratify the appointment to a lectureship of a German who boasted of friendly contacts with the Baader-Meinhof gang. There is no getting away from it, he thought as he passed up the narrow street that led from the Casa back to the Plaza Mayor of the old town, she would not hesitate to do me harm — if the opportunity was presented to her in a politically attractive way.

And there, on the corner by the side entrance to the cathedral was the SEAT 127 that had followed his taxi from the hotel, and there, coming out of the café opposite the Casa de Colón, was the tall man in a dark, almost black suit, who had been driving it. Well, he knew his job, for he turned away from Argand, walked briskly off the other way. Grade three surveillance — it was important for the watcher to remain unrecognizable and at a distance, even at the risk of losing the subject. Either that or he had a back-up Argand had failed so far to spot.

57

He walked round two sides of the dull, dark square in which each building seemed to be a government office of some sort, until he came to the portico of the *Gran Cabildo Insular*, the seat of local government. The pamphlets in his case had told him that since Franco's death the islands had been granted a real measure of autonomy in local affairs, though defence, fiscal matters and finance, subsidies from the mainland, and so on remained in the hands of the metropolitan ministries. He looked up at the frieze above the pillars. Six well-draped ladies clustered around a central figure who was offering her breast to a baby. *Maxima est Caritas*: seven virtues and the greatest of these is Charity.

The SEAT on the other side of the square remained empty and Argand got into a taxi from the rank beneath the colonnade.

The sudden dusk of the subtropics had descended by the time he reached the Santa Teresa. The Yacht Club, a palace of glass, glowed like something newly arrived from space, the wavelets in the marina flashed back its reflection. The Santa Teresa itself was floodlit — a white colonial façade surrounded by lawns and palms, all acid green in the lights.

Inside there was a definite if subdued atmosphere of excitement — anticipation at any rate. The bars were filling up, guests moving about, the servants fresh and willing, the air most delicately tainted with kitchen odours. Argand hesitated, not wanting to go up to the blank boredom of his room, thinking that for once a pre-prandial sherry might be no bad thing, but not wanting to go to a bar. He never, except in the line of duty, drank in bars. To the side of the hotel, occupying a built-on wing, was an orangery, laid out with wicker chairs and citrus trees growing in handsome ceramic pots. It looked attractive. Argand found a chair and table near the far end, a waiter appeared promptly and took his order — Tío Pepe and nuts. He sipped and sat there, wondering what to do about the man or men who were following him. The point was, like Salim and Brunot they were a lead, they could be turned round, could give him the line he needed to trace the plot against him back to its origin. And after the fiasco at the Casa de Colón he had determined to leave Brunot and Salim until he had something more concrete to go on. The CRIC files he had telexed for had not yet arrived.

A laugh, loud and braying, caught his attention, and by shifting in his seat (the cane creaked) and peering past the heavy foliage of the lemon trees he could see its source, a man Argand instantly recognized. He was tall and very thin; wore a navy blazer with brass buttons embossed with some military insignia or other; his face, beneath straw hair, was cadaverous: pale blue eyes glinted in grey sockets, two deep lines outlined a long, very long chin. Trencher. Commander Trencher. Metz '77, the Arms Fair. Argand had been part of a Brabanter delegation buying IS *matériel* and anti-terrorist devices; Trencher, a salesman, working for an English firm. He was a bore and a drunk. Argand was about to pull back, not wishing to be recognized, when Trencher moved and revealed the face of the man he was with.

This time Argand took a moment to place him. The sleek, silver hair, the slate-blue suit, a knitted black tie, then, as he turned, the clover-leaf mark on the neck beneath the ear. It was the bank official, manager or whatever, who had supervised the removal of cash and notes from the Banco de Santa Caridad that morning. Interesting that he was doing business with Trencher — but not necessarily surprising. Or rather – *not* doing business, for the banker looked angry, confused or embarrassed — it was difficult to say which. And Trencher laughed again, then shook his head — a definite refusal. The banker stood up, took something from the open document case on the table in front of him — it looked like a large brochure — and almost tossed it behind an orange tree.

Clearly he was in a temper. Trencher rose too, unfolding barely articulated limbs until his chin was above the banker's head. Argand pulled back as they came past, hoping Trencher would not spot him, but Trencher did, paused, a question in his grey face, and then raised a long finger in recognition before continuing on his way behind the banker.

All of which was enough for Argand. Better to eat out, see some more of the town, perhaps, if he was lucky, get behind his tail, than stay put and risk sharing a meal and the evening with the cadaverous Englishman.

He walked. The evening was warm, balmy, the streets crowded. Tourists, sailors in shabby but neat suits, ordinary working people — the men in white shirts, the girls in pretty dresses — sauntered along the boulevards gawping at the treasures in the brightly lit shops, most of which remained open. It was going to be difficult to spot a tail as early as this, better surely to find somewhere to eat, wait for the crowds to thin. But none of the restaurants appealed to him — in the area near the Santa Teresa they were all very expensive, very pretentious. He walked on. The area changed abruptly: the streets were narrower, darker, though still modern and ugly. There were more bars now, squalid little places each with one long counter leaving a gap barely wide enough to stand in between it and the window, and each with at least three noisy pinball machines. He was too near the port — a sudden whiff of poisonously heavy scent from a narrow doorway and a glimpse of thigh beneath a cheap fur confirmed this, and he turned abruptly, thinking to retrace his steps.

And at fifty metres a blue jacket beneath a dark head twisted away too; Argand almost ran to the spot, pushing past a group arguing and spitting round a girl who was distributing pamphlets about the Base, but the man had gone — at least was nowhere to be seen.

Argand went on more slowly, more warily, his mind now only half on finding somewhere to eat, yet forcing himself not to repeat the silly, unconsidered manoeuvre. He'd get behind the man all right when things were quieter, meanwhile he must be patient.

A restaurant at last caught his eye. It was no *Louis Bonaparte*, which was the place where he always ate at home in Brabt, this being shabby and brightly lit; but it looked honest enough, was doing a fair trade with a respectable-looking clientéle. Argand went in and caught a glimpse again, reflected in the glass door as he opened it, of the dark figure in the blue jacket, on the other side of the road now, peering after him.

His meal was not a success. There was no wienerschnitzel and the waiter took him for a tourist, spoke English of a sort, insisted on choosing his menu for him: all the dishes would be *muy típico*, the cuisine of the islands was famous, *no, no señor*, not expensive, certainly not, the island people were poor, knew how to make the best of plain ingredients.

He ate: a plate of small potatoes, barely bigger than large peas, boiled unpeeled and served with a paprika sauce that was far too hot; a sort of dry pâté, bitter in taste, the basic constituent of which seemed to be millet, served with a tiny glass of yellow rum, *muy típico, señor*; *sancocho*, a stew of tough, salted fish, which was the *piéce de résistance* and quite foul; and finally, for dessert, an over-ripe banana — he refused guavas. He drank, apart from the rum, a half carafe of sweet metallic-tasting wine from Santa Templanza, a Virtue apparently entirely covered with lava, where holes for the vines had to be hacked through the thin rock to the soil beneath. It was, the waiter insisted, not only *muy típico* but *muy bueno* as well.

He left in a bad temper, after noting that most of the locals were eating pork chops, and almost immediately saw the dark figure in the blue jacket rise from a pavement café across the road. He now realized what had not occurred to him before, that the man on his tail was Salim Tumbal Robertson, the half-breed who had planted

61

the heroin on him in the first place. Frustration, dyspepsia, and a feeling that he might at last gain control of events instead of being at the mercy of them, played on a mind still convalescent from depression and fatigue (rather than paranoid schizophrenia) to produce a steady burn of anger.

A hundred metres away bright light spilled on to a crowd, silhouetting them sharply, leaving the details dark. A cinema perhaps. People waiting to go in. Argand quickened his pace, pushed into the group, scarcely taking in that it was entirely composed of prostitutes and pimps, that the cinema was showing an *Emmanuelle* film, and that they were waiting for the sailors inside to come out. He ducked into the next doorway beyond. This was also well lit, was the foyer of a rooming house or whatever; a painted woman, burly, beetle-browed, sat on the third stair from the bottom with her skirt round her waist and her legs apart. She looked pleased to see the Brabanter Commissioner for Public Order.

Salim hesitated on the threshold, Argand grabbed for his arm, caught it, and swung the small man into the hallway with him, for a second catching again the smell of stale spice; then the Indian broke free and ran, past Argand and up the stairs. Argand caught him on the second landing and bundled him through an open door into a small, grubby bathroom. One heavy push sent the small man, little more than a youth really, into the bath, and there he lay, doubled up, with his legs hanging over the edge, his eyes wild and bloodshot, his mouth open and gasping. Argand fought to get his breath back too.

At last, though still gasping, he said: "You are Salim Tumbal Robertson?"

The Indian nodded, quickly, three times.

"Right Salim. Who sent you, who sent you, eh?"

The head went down again, swayed to and fro in a gesture of

despair, like a caged animal's. Argand took hold of his hair and yanked.

"You planted that heroin on me. Didn't you? You planted it on me. Answer me."

"Yes. Yes, sir, that's right. I did. I swapped the cases. It was me. I don't deny it."

"So who sent you? Whose idea was it?"

"No one's idea, sir. No one. Just me, sir."

Argand hit him quite hard, backhanded across his left ear, and for a minute or more could get nothing out of Salim except gasping, retching sobs.

"Who are you working for? Come on. Who is the boss?"

"I work for Joachim, sir. My stepfather. Since he married my mother I am working for Joachim. He is, sir, a very respected trader, I assure you . . ."

Argand hit him again.

The voice rose to a whine: "A respected trader, sir. Never in drugs, never in drugs at all."

There are techniques for resisting questioning, ways of side-tracking the line of interrogation into safe areas, of assuming ignorance in others. An adept may be as skilful with them as an experienced interrogator is with the tools of his own side of the trade. Argand sensed that Joachim, whoever he might be, was a dead end, at least for the present. Salim was obviously ready to catalogue every item that his stepfather had ever handled. He switched to another line.

"Right, Salim. You made sure I got your case with the heroin."

"Yes, sir."

"And my case went to Brunot."

"Brunot?" Salim's face was beginning to look puffy, but could still register shifts of emotion. Doubt had changed to surprise. "That is the name of the lady in the university residence? Yes, sir.

She it is has your case. You want your case you ask her for it; believe me, sir. She has your case. . . ."

This too was a transparent attempt at sidetracking, impudent even, and Argand hit him again. The bones between his knuckles and the top of his wrist jarred quite painfully.

"Heaven and hell, Salim, I want the truth, you hear me. Now give me no more answers like that, just the truth, the whole story. So. Who gave you the case with the heroin. The truth, Salim. Who gave it to you?"

The blood from his mouth was coming faster now, and the body rocked to and fro. Argand raised his hand again, and Salim cringed away beneath it. The words came thick and slurred, but coherent enough.

"Don't hit me no more, sir, don't hit me no more. I tell you all, I promise I tell you all. First it was to be routine, sir. Just as usual. I pick up the case in the 'self' at the airport. It is left there by the table nearest the counter, by the door, each time I have to be there exactly at that time. But this time everything is different. A man is there to give it to me and the case is different, larger, heavier, but everything else is right, so I take it. On the plane I open it. That also is usual with me, but this time I see heroin. So I am very frightened. And then there will be a search at Barajas, so when I have the chance, in the time when all are frightened, I take your case, and you take mine . . . ."

"But how did you know this was what you had to do? Where were the instructions telling you to do this?"

"No instructions, sir, in emergency it was what was arranged for me."

In the face of this nonsense Argand's control went completely and with both hands clenched together he swung at the brown man's head as if he held a pickaxe. Salim rolled away as the blow came, ducking out of its line, and as the back of Argand's already

64

sore hand smashed into one of the taps he twisted away like a cat that doesn't want to be held any more, out of the bath, and leaped for the door. The shock of severe pain froze Argand for one blind second, and it was enough. Salim was off before Argand could grab him, pelting down the stairs with the policeman after him. But as Argand turned the corner he ran straight into the arms of the burly beetle-browed prostitute and she held on, held him in a hug with hands fastened behind his back. By the time Argand was free Salim had gone, out in the street there was no sign of him.

With the curses of the prostitute and the jeers of her colleagues and their men ringing in his ears Argand broke away and strode off towards the brighter lights he had left, and the security of the Santa Teresa.

His main feeling when he got back was self-disgust. Twice that day he had lost control, twice he had been overcome by waves of irrational and powerful emotion. For a man of Argand's character this was deeply humiliating, and a humiliated man does not like to be alone. Although it was now almost deserted he preferred the orangery to his own room — and because he did not like to sit there without ordering he sent for whisky and water. Gradually he got his feelings under control and began once more to look around him, aware that lonely though he was he did not want to run into Trencher.

He was now further in than he had been before. The brochure, or whatever, that the banker had thrown away still lay where it had fallen behind the ceramic tub. Argand could see an advertisement for Peter Stuyvesant on the back. Not then, a brochure. Without really thinking why, he pulled it out and turned it over. A red-head in stockings and nothing else smiled up at him from satin cushions. He had time, just, to turn her over again before the waiter arrived with his drink.

VIII

"I THOUGHT you ought to see it," said Pérez. "See the size of the problem."

The Mercedes pitched and rolled over cobbles and rails, threaded through a complex of warehouses and offices, and so came on to the main quay of Las Guavas port, a straight avenue of cranes and container hoists. To their left the bay curved back to the old town — hotels, clubs, beaches, and the Yacht Club marina gleamed beguilingly in the fresh morning sun; a pair of water skiers cut white wounds in the water. In front of them, at the far end of the quay, yet already filling the view through the windscreen, stood the giant digger.

It was as big as a church and looked like nothing so much as a load of fairground equipment that had been crushed together and dumped in a scrap-yard. In front was a big wheel, ten metres in diameter and hung with enormous clawed buckets instead of gondolas, behind lay a weird conglomeration of engines, cabins, pipes, chimneys, cylinders, belts and chains, the whole lot mounted on giant tracks nearly three metres high. It was alive — or seemed to be. It pushed puffs of black smoke out from two or three different vents, the air above its flues shimmered and bent in the heat that rose from deep in its intestines, it purred in places, clanked in others, and it smelled of oil, grease, diesel and dirt. It dwarfed completely the white Rolls-Royce that was parked in front of it and the three men who stood waiting on the edge of the quay. Pérez placed the Mercedes by the Rolls and as he did so

Argand realized that he knew two of the men and could guess who the third was. Sam Peters, yes, and the silver-haired banker who had been with Trencher in the Santa Teresa; the third must be Pérez's father-in-law — a tall, large man, leonine with longish grey hair, a coat like a cape across his shoulders. As he got out, Argand noticed that the Rolls had a fresh dent on the right wing.

Pérez performed perfunctory introductions, the banker — Enrique Cortés — and Salvador Guzmán briefly touched Argand's hand, then Guzmán took Pérez to one side, his arm round his shoulder, talking earnestly, quickly in Spanish. Cortés joined in. Argand knew enough to catch one phrase and that, he assumed, about him — *no habla español*, he doesn't speak Spanish.

"Impressive, yes?" said Peters, at his shoulder.

"The digger or Guzmán?"

Peters laughed. "Oh sure, both. But I meant the digger. Ugly, but a technological marvel. French. It has four engines, something goes wrong every half hour, it needs an oil well all to itself to fuel it. But by God it shifts shit, it sure can shift shit." He took Argand by the arm and led him away from the others, away from the digger. "Guzmán is impressive too but not at his fresh, crisp, newly-baked best today."

Argand was not sure that he had found much to admire in Guzmán. His first feeling was that here was a man on the edge of decay — the face greyish and fleshy, the hair a touch lank, the eyes, which were a startling blue, rheumy, though that may have been from the stiffish breeze that blew off the ocean. Certainly he looked worried, needed to tell Pérez whatever it was he had to say as quickly as possible.

Peters chatted on: "Nevertheless he is a swell, the real thing, straight off Nob Hill, know what I mean? There's English aristo blood via the Argentine and his wife's a third cousin to the Albas. And you should see his finca. They say Franco spent his honeymoon there, though if that was true of every place they said it of he'd never have had time to save the *Patria* from socialism. Anyway, not at his best today, Guzmán I mean. The old order meets the new, get it?"

"I'm not sure I do."

"That," said Peters, indicating the monster behind them with a lift of his head, "is the principal reason why father-in-law's companies didn't get the chief contract for the Base. That and their reputation for using dummy cement like on the airport runway. IBOBRAS with EUROSTRUCT behind them could base their tender on the assumption that they could hire that, EUROSTRUCT are part owners, and it's going to cut their labour costs by more than a third. That's a lot of dough these days, especially now cheap labour in old España is a thing of the past."

"I understood Guzmán has been sub-contracted for a lot of the work."

"Sure. As much as he can handle I daresay. All the same. Hey. I think we're about to be granted an audience."

The three Spaniards were coming down the quay towards them, Guzmán in front with a smile that may have been meant to be ingratiating.

This time he spoke English: "Commissioner, my son-in-law has a problem. He tells me that you are going to help him with it."

"You mean getting the digger on to the site?"

"Tell us Commissioner, your frank opinion, is it possible?" The big head on one side, the smile quizzical, disinterested. Did the contractor really care one way or another? Argand distrusted his easy urbanity.

He bit his thumbnail. "In the face of a large, organized demonstration, no. But how long have you got?"

"IBOBRAS say they must have it digging within a week. And it's the Cabildo's responsibility to get it on to the site. There's no indemnity clause that says so. After one week any hold-up due to

68

civil disturbance becomes a charge on the islands. You must understand I am speaking as Chairman of the Public Works Committee," the smile widened, "and not as a major contractor."

"You bet your sweet fanny you are." Peters was suddenly almost vicious. Guzmán looked taken aback. "So just what are you going to do about it? Have you worked out just how much the daily hire of this baby is going to cost?"

For a moment they looked at each other, Pérez, Peters, Guzmán, faces like masks, mouths set, and Argand looked on, excluded from a storm of feeling that enclosed the three of them. Then Peters shrugged. "Oh shit," he said, "I guess you know where it's at. Carry on. Don't mind me."

Enrique Cortés, the silver-haired banker, suddenly intervened; he spoke rapidly, with venom, and short, sharp, emphatic gestures. Pérez expostulated, protested, Guzmán looked thoughtful. Peters took the match-stalk he was chewing out of his mouth and flicked it away. A gull deviated from its progress towards some garbage floating in the slack water beneath them, then thought better of it, and went on.

"Señor Cortés," he said, "is of the opinion that we should land a regiment of legionaries. He reckons they'd see the digger through all right. Señor Pérez dissents. He is sure the Governor would never give them leave to land. Señor Guzmán thinks he might. I agree, especially if say Commissioner Argand, the greatest IS expert in the West said it was the only way."

Argand frowned. "It would be madness. At least on the day of the strike . . ." He was aware that they were all now listening to him, Cortés leaning forward like someone deaf and asking Pérez to translate at times. Argand had little respect for him, a businessman who carried girlie magazines in his case, and went briskly on with what he had to say. "You already have a general strike called for the day scheduled for the move . . ."

"There'd be a massacre."

69

"With professional soldiers used to combat, yes."

"Rivers of blood. Bad PR. So what do you suggest? Cancel the scheduled move?"

"No. I think you should start, provoke a confrontation, and then step down."

Pérez frowned. "You mean once they see they've achieved something they'll go home. But as soon as we try again the same thing . . ."

"Not necessarily. Look. At the moment everyone's against this thing. No one wants it. The extreme left against the Base don't want it; the construction workers . . ."

"And San Salvador SA doesn't want it. Sure as hell it's a pain in the ass for San Salvador."

Argand sniffed deeply, clenched his fists in his pockets, and half turned from the American, ignoring him. Guzmán, however, remained bland.

"No one wants it, so everyone will be pleased when we back down." He hesitated for a moment, hearing again the way he had said "we". "Right. Then start negotiations. Talk to the Union. Offer limited overmanning concessions, details to be worked out later. I'm sure you have contingency plans for pulling in the leaders of this Junta against the Base, so round them up. Then move it at night. How long will it take? Six hours? Move it at night."

Pérez scratched the thinning hair on top of his head. "Not at night," he said. "It has to go through the area where the dockers live. The poorer ones are immigrants, from the Sahara. Not as radicalized as the left likes to think, but they would certainly welcome a chance, an excuse to get out on the streets at night."

Argand shrugged. "Is there a day that would do as well? A holiday, a feast day, a day when people would be elsewhere?"

"There is. Four days away, the eighth of September, Our Lady's

70

Nativity. Half the population make the *romería* to Nuestra Señora de Las Guavas, to her shrine the other side of San Cristóbal. But that day we are fully stretched, I'll have no police to spare to see this through the centre of town. And the garrison parades at the shrine too. Anyway, as you know, I can't rely on them if the Union does get out a strong picket in spite of everything."

They had walked some way down the quay now, away from the monster and towards the container park. A corner of Argand's mind wondered if Trencher's wares, whatever he was in Las Guavas to sell, were in there amongst the rest. The four men stopped, turned inwards to face each other. The wind ruffled Peters' greasy hair, lifted the lapels of his untidy jacket.

"Sure," he said, "but as Señor Enrique has reminded us — there's always the Legion."

"*Sí, sí señor, claro*, there is always the Legion." This time the banker had followed what was said well enough, though probably he had missed most of what had gone before.

Pérez turned, eyebrows lifted, a frown hovering, or was the reaction deeper? Again Argand sensed a tension he could not explain.

"Perhaps the Governor would allow the Legion to land on a day when there were no other forces available. And just to see that thing on to the site. I should explain," he went on, to Argand, "the Legion used to join this parade, but last year there was fighting afterwards between conscripts and legionaries. Since then the Governor has banned the presence of the Legion on Santa Caridad, except in very small numbers on furlough. But it's worth a try. I could approach him."

"Now why don't you do that?" said Peters. "It could be announced they were coming for their usual blessing at the shrine, they were all heartbroken about last year, they want to make amends, they'll shoot themselves if they are kept away. The

71

Archbishop could guarantee their good behaviour, say they should come, their souls need it . . ."

Guzmán smiled. "I know His Reverence. He is a personal friend. I'm sure I can ask him to do that."

"Of course he will. Now tell me, Commissioner, how many legionaries would you reckon?"

"That's difficult to say. I shall have to go over the ground. And know what equipment they have, how well trained they are in this sort of operation . . . ."

"Sure. But make a guess, an informed estimate. Update it later if you want, but put a figure on it now. A battalion? Would five hundred be enough?"

"Five hundred at least. Say five hundred plus support units."

There was an unexplained excitement in Peters' voice as he went on. "So this is the scenario as I see it. We make a dummy attempt to shift that junk the day after tomorrow as scheduled. And when it gets rough we jack it in. Then Pérez goes to the Governor with Jan's plan here for the eighth. That is the plan of the greatest IS expert in the West. The garrison, the Union, Pérez's police are all up at the shrine singing happy birthday to her ladyship, and everyone is expecting five hundred legionaries to turn up too, because the Archbishop has said they should. But they just stay down here in Las Guavas and provide a guard of honour for old juggernaut instead. Is that about it? Have I got it right?"

He took silence for assent.

"Right then, Commissioner. You'll do an *aide-mémoire* for the Governor. We'll work on it together and Pérez can put in the accents for me, get in all the *ilustrísimos* and *excelentísimos* the old bird will expect. It'll work like a dream, you'll see. Up at the shrine they'll all be so relieved the Legion hasn't turned up after all, they'll not be worrying very much about what they are doing down here. . . ."

72

He turned away, back towards the digger. They watched him for a moment, fat-arsed beneath his crumpled jacket.

Then Pérez said: "I think we have come up with the best plan. Especially if we can persuade the Governor to let the Legion handle it. It is important for me that my men retain what support they do get from the public."

"Of course. One cannot over-emphasize the importance of that." Argand was a touch pompous over this, the way men used to authority are when they want to push home what to them is indisputable.

Guzmán turned to him, took his hand. "I think your personal recommendation to the Governor could be crucial. He has the highest respect for you, I know. Come on Enrique, we must be off now. I'm so glad we've sorted all this out. It was embarrassing for me, you understand, people might think I was obstructing the use of the digger for my own ends. Far from it, far from it. . . . I'm sure we'll meet again. Perhaps in my place out of town, yes indeed. I'll see you receive an invitation. Come on now Enrique, we still have a lot to see to."

He shook hands, the banker did too.

Peters, Pérez and Argand watched as the enormous white car purred into life and slid away down the quay. The driver was a young man, not uniformed, with a hard, almost cruel face.

Peters said: "He shouldn't let Carlos drive that monster, he really shouldn't. He terrifies me."

Pérez agreed: "Me too. But what can we do? Salvador has always spoiled him, always will." He turned to Argand. "Carlos is his only son. Illegitimate of course. So . . ." he shrugged.

It did not occur to Argand to ask why Carlos should not drive. Things would have turned out differently perhaps if he had, but by now he had had enough of Guzmán and his family.

They had lunch at the Yacht Club. As they were eating their

73

shrimps Pérez said: "By the way, we picked up your Salim last night. Someone had been knocking him about . . . ."

Peters butted in. "You mean Jan's accomplice in heroin smuggling? Hey Jan, I bet you beat him up. He let you down, so you roughed him about a little, I guess."

Argand went white, had to struggle for control. At last he asked, "What will you do with him?"

Pérez seemed not to have noticed anything wrong.

"Hold him for a day then turn him loose again. He won't crack, and we've nothing really to pin on him." He stabbed at one of the tiny crustaceans on his plate. "He's a petty crook. Free ports attract them. Not important so long as they keep to themselves. I just thought you'd like to know. The wienerschnitzel is for you, isn't it? They do a good one here."

Later they drove over the route the digger would have to take. Argand felt a little better. After the shock of the news about Salim he had taken a small dose of Dr Liszt's tranquillizer. At the dock-gates pickets were already out, some five or six hundred now, men in workers' blues, students, girls too. There were banners and placards. To get through Pérez had to switch on his siren and even then the wings of the Mercedes were banged and a girl risked her life trying to put a pamphlet under the wipers.

They turned right into Avenida de Venezuela.

"It will have to come down here," said Pérez, "it's the only road wide enough across the isthmus. We'll close it on the day, on the eighth, and on the day of the strike too. I shall have to see that an announcement is made on Radio Popular de Las Guavas. There is still a lot to be worked out. This roundabout is a vulnerable point. There will be a quite complicated manoeuvre, the engineers reckon twenty minutes . . . Dios, now what?"

74

At the far end of the street — they could see the ocean beyond — there were flashing lights, blue and orange, and then nearer the banshee howl of a siren. Pérez picked up the handset of the radio. Voices crackled, he switched on their siren, then accelerated away so that Argand had to clutch for the crash handle.

"There have been bank raids," Pérez shouted above the din. "Three. No details yet but there has been some shooting." He gave a sharp laugh. "It's a bit much, eh? Isn't that what they say? A bit much. On top of all the rest."

IX

INFO req input 86794371 rec 2237 020980
Info req output 87694371/1 del 0059 030980
Subjs Joachim Joachim / Salim Tumbal Robertson
Joachim Joachim Male Born 170318 Macau Portuguese Passport.
Pre hab Av. Venezuela 8/4E Las Guavas Santa Caridad Las
Virtudes Espana. Mar: Lilak Tumbal Robertson, wid (Prev mar
Sgt. Albert Robertson, one son Salim see seq.). No known child.
No known convictions.
Joachim Joachim arrived Lisbon from Mozambique 1/68; moved
to Gibraltar (marriage above) 4/70; moved to present address 5/72.
Believed to own real estate Cap d'Agde, France 1100. Pres. Occ.
Gem dealing.
Comment: Illegal trafficking in gems and gold suspected since
8/68; Dutch investigation 7/77 negative; known contacts (legal)
Amsterdam, London, New York, Bangkok, Hongkong, Macau.
Previous requests for info from A80965, 7/79, 11/79.

The computer printout rustled dryly as Argand folded the top
portion under and began on the second; the basketwork of the
chair he was sitting in creaked in response. Someone coughed
nearby, and he peered up through the fan-like foliage of the
delicate palm plant that grew out of a white and yellow ceramic tub
by the side of his chair. On the other side of the room, a wide
lounge this time, silhouetted against leaded windows decorated
with stained glass depicting girls picking guavas and artificially lit

from behind, he now made out the profile, sharp and angular, of Trencher. He was surprised he had not heard him arrive — it was well past midnight and the hotel was quiet, much of it in near darkness or at any rate lit dimly. A waiter glided silently across the tiled floor to the Englishman's elbow, took a whispered order, and glided on. When he was gone Trencher raised a finger in acknowledgement of Argand's presence, and then, as he unfolded an airmail edition of *The Times*, the loudest noise yet crackled briefly about the spaces of the room. Argand returned to the printout.

Salim Tumbal Robertson. Male Born 150952 Gibraltar. UK passport, no right of residence. Single. Hab: C. Cervantes 33/Atico dra, Las Guavas. No known child.
Prev. convictions: shoplifting, 181268, fined; cannabis possession 160670, one year suspended. Apply Gibraltar police for further info.
Occupation: Employed by Joachim Joachim. Duties: Clerk and courier.
Comment: Mother, widow, married Joachim Joachim, see above. Moved with parent from Gibraltar to Las Guavas 5/72. Almost certainly has acted illegally as courier in gem smuggling operations. Between 5/78 and 6/79 made eight trips to Tehran.
Prev. req. for info from A80965, 7/79, 11/79.

It didn't amount to much, added little really to what Argand had already pieced together from what Salim had let out on the previous evening and what Pérez had had to say about them. No doubt Salim was a crook, no doubt his stepfather was too — but a skilful operator and successful. Real estate on the Mediterranean coast of France was not cheap. Still there were the addresses. Tomorrow, in the afternoon, he would have an opportunity to call on one or the other, clearly that was the next line to take.

The cannabis conviction was revealing. It was unlikely the Gibraltar police would press for a prison sentence, even suspended, for possession only — but if they thought Salim had been trafficking . . . And of course if Salim had been in touch with cannabis dealers ten years ago, when he was only eighteen, then might he not be in heroin by now? Though it was unlikely that his stepfather was — the CRIC report would have recorded it, even the slightest suspicion.

The previous requests were interesting too. Argand pulled out his little black book. Yes. The prefix A809 indicated an American agency. Unfortunately the 65 remained unexplained. A pity — he would have liked to know just which agency was interested in Joachim and Salim. The trips to Tehran were an indicator perhaps. The flow of both gems and drugs from Iran as the Shah's government began to topple had been a matter of concern in Europe — no doubt the Americans had been worried as well.

He folded down the printout to the next item.

Info req input 87694371/P rec 2237/020980
Info req output 87694371/P2 del 0059 030980
Subj Françoise Brunot . . .

The waiter stooped at his ear.

"Excuse me, sir. Commander Trencher wonders if you would care to join him for a night-cap."

Argand glanced up, across the darkened archipelago of wicker furniture. The Englishman's shoulder lifted — a question, but take it or leave it. Argand was tempted to leave it, but he was curious about Trencher's presence in Las Guavas. He folded the flimsy printouts into his inside pocket and followed the waiter across. Trencher rose as he came, unfolded his long, very thin limbs, held out limp fingers.

"Commissioner. We have met, I believe."

"Yes. Metz. Autumn '77."

"It seems like me you suffer from insomnia. Would you join me in a night-cap? I have a very good recipe if you would like to try it. A sort of toddy."

In fair Spanish he ordered whisky, fresh lemon, warm water. When the waiter returned he stirred in a spoonful of honey from a small pot in front of him. "Dorset," he said. "Lime and clover. You may well find it sends you off. I never travel without it. Cheers."

They drank.

"Still in the same line of business, Commissioner?"

Argand explained briefly why he was in Las Guavas.

"Then you'll know my good friend Salvador Guzmán. He's up to all sorts of tricks, but at least it's no secret that his is the biggest construction firm on the island."

"And you're selling IS *matériel* to the Cabildo?" Argand put the question out of politeness rather than interest.

"Is that what you have been told?"

"No, no. I'm afraid it's just a conclusion I jumped to."

"No. Nothing official about my visit at all. Of course it is business. I don't suppose anyone pays their own bills in places like this any more." The limp hand flapped across his wrist, leaving the palm up, the fingers outstretched. It seemed Trencher was too tired or too bored to do anything about it, and he left it hanging there over the arm of the chair. "Except filmstars and pop singers," he added.

They sipped. Argand found the drink pleasant, settling. The silence stretched and then folded itself around them. Only very distantly could they hear a woman's voice quietly singing, the clink of cutlery and china. A lift whirred smoothly.

"Mind you, the way things are going I shan't hang on here much

79

longer. My principals are the most accommodating people imaginable, but they do like some return for what they have laid out, and I rather think we have been let down on this particular deal." Pale eyes set in wide circles of grey skin peered across the table at Argand. "Chinks just not as readily forthcoming as we had been led to believe, don't you know," he drawled, and at last the hand was brought in to flop on the edge of the table where the finger ends picked at a loose bit of wicker. "Can't give much in the way of credit in this line, you know?"

Argand felt he was meant to say something.

"It is still the same line, then?" he offered.

"More or less. More or less. *Matériel*. Free port, you see. Warehouse it here, reasonable charges, deeds of ownership, exchange contracts, bills of lading. Local banks lend a hand, they know the business. Of course we never know who we're dealing with, not officially. Wouldn't do if we did. Not our business who uses the stuff. But they always want credit, offer the wildest terms imaginable. The way they see it, come the revolution or whatever, they'll have unlimited funds, no problem, pay off everybody a hundred fold. The way we see it is — what if the revolution fails? The few thousand or whatever they owe us will be the least of their worries when they're on the end of a firing squad. So cash on the nail is our rule, let some other poor bugger do the financing." He paused and shook his cadaverous head. "And cash on the nail seems just not to be forthcoming in this particular case after all."

"Tiresome for you."

"Damned nuisance. All set up. Local businessman guaranteeing letters of credit, sum on deposit local bank, negotiable in London, and then for some reason the blighter backs out. Spot more?"

"No thanks."

"Think I will." But Trencher didn't signal for the waiter — he topped up his glass from a silver pocket flask. Argand watched more carefully. The lip of the flask tinkled against the rim of the glass, the hand that lifted it shook. Trencher, he remembered, was a drunk. Argand had wondered why he had been invited over, why Trencher was so ready to gossip — now he knew. Trencher would want company until he was almost on the edge of oblivion.

"Yes. It's all here you know. Sitting in the bonded part of the port. Whole container full. That's the damned nuisance of it. Got to ship it back out if we don't sell it here. Always find a market of course. Find one just like that. But m' principals are just a touch fussy since poor ol' Lord Louis. American Irish dollars just not so acceptable as they were. Not for a time anyway. Understandable. But damned inconvenient." He gave a meaningless little splutter, not quite a laugh. "Ah well. Not to worry. I'll give this lot another twenty-four hours anyway. They may still come up with the ante after all."

He drained his glass, screwed down the top on his honey jar and stood up. Only the way he tucked *The Times* under his arm — almost in the armpit and slightly tilted — showed how far gone he was.

"Time for bed. See you around for a day or two? Good. I like to think there's a chap I can chat to, one gets a little lonely in these places, don't you find?"

Argand watched his slow but steady progress across the floor. Only once did he nudge one of the tables. In the lit entrance to the hall, he turned, gave a half wave and swayed ever so slightly with it, then was gone. Argand heard the whisper of the lift door, the whirr of cables. He unfolded the computer printout again. It had not occurred to him to question why Trencher had brought up the name of Salvador Guzmán.

Françoise Brunot. Female. Born 130150. Hab: Viktorhugostras 17/6 Brabt 3. Single. No known child.
Convictions: Unlawful assembly, 5/68, fine; wilful damage to

public property 6/68, fine; assaulting officer of State Security Police, 8/72, six months suspended.

Affiliations: League of Socialist Youth; International Association of Marxist Teachers; SHREW.

Occupation: Lecturer in Spanish, Brabt University.

Comment: Investigated by State Security Police 9/75; grade 2 surveillance 2/77 — 4/78 under anti-terrorist laws. No charges brought. Frequently takes lovers, but attachments rarely last more than six months. If necessary could be held under Section 183, para 4 (Leg XVII, '98).

Section 183 of the Brabanter penal code demanded exemplary standards of moral behaviour from all state-employed teachers. It was rarely invoked but remained on the statute books, ostensibly because any attempt to remove it was resisted in the Brabanter Moot by the small but influential group of Protestant members. In fact the authorities used it as a means for dismissing incompetent teachers with security of tenure, and for dealing with political dissidents.

Argand's emotions as he came to the end of this were powerful and equivocal. Suddenly he had a strong sense of the girl's presence — not a vision exactly, but yet she was *there*, very strongly so, and the experience produced a sweat in his palms and a strong, involuntary shudder. Stocky, but by no means plump, wide-browed, large-eyed, brunette, plainly dressed, no make-up, energetic, lively, good-humoured he suspected, strong-willed, intelligent — how was it, how could it be that all this, *this* . . . was true about her. What had gone wrong with the girl, woman? She was obviously fit in every possible way to live out a good wholesome life as mother and wife, working alongside the sort of yeomen farmers who were, on his mother's side, Argand's own forbears. Why should she end up drifting from layabout to layabout (the youth in fitted denims he had seen her with became a presence too), doing a pointless job, and actually conspiring with a gang of lefties like the IAMT, and women's libbers like SHREW to destroy the society of which she could have been such an ornament, such a pillar.

He pulled out his handkerchief, wiped his palms and his brow, looked almost guiltily around the wide deserted lounge, wondering if anyone had been there to witness the emotion that had suddenly distracted him. Then he carefully folded away the printouts and stood up. One thing at any rate was clear, quite clear. His worst suspicions were justified — the fact that someone as clearly inimical to him as Brunot had got hold of his case was no coincidence — it would be the height of foolishness to suppose it was.

He made his way slowly up the stairs to his room — Argand rarely took a lift if he could reasonably walk. The hotel remained silent around him — it was now well after one o'clock. The corridors were in almost complete darkness apart from red safety lights that glowed over each landing and intersection. His feet were soundless on the deep carpets. The large key made no noise in his door but the thick heavy metal tag on the end clanked solidly against the wood. Cool air with the ocean ozone on it breathed out of the dark across his forehead, and he remembered that his last action on leaving had been to shut the window.

He reached for the light switch with his left hand as he came through the door and swung the weighted key with the other. The shadow ducked away from the key and came in low before he could get to the light, gripping him by the waist and carrying him to the ground where his head struck a projecting corner of the skirting board. Momentarily dazed he lay there and the obscene embrace tightened, crushing the breath from his lungs while a practised knee felt for his groin. He caught a whiff of stale garlic, of sour armpits, then twisted an elbow free which he jabbed as hard as he could at the point where he judged the corner of his attacker's jaw would be. The hold relaxed for a second, Argand twisted again, this time on to his back, and felt the grip shift but the long arms snaked up under his armpits, hands came round and locked beneath his chin. The full weight of the man was now on his chest, the knee had found his groin, the lock on his neck was lethal — a sharp jerk could dislocate his vertebrae, steady pressure would suffocate him.

Argand was a trained policeman and his reactions were instinctive. The only way to break the hold, which forces a submission in wrestling, was to use the one countermeasure wrestlers are forbidden. The palms of his hands slid to the man's face, pushed into nylon, and his strong thumbs, braced to exert maximum pressure, dug towards the inner corners of the eyesockets. One thumb found the softness beneath the nylon hood and dug, the other still encountered hardness for a second, but enough had been done — with a gasp that had terror in it as well as pain the pressure was released and Argand jerked the top of his head into the man's neck and heaved at the same time.

Resistance swiftly melted to nothing in the darkness, and then briefly, still on all fours and gasping for breath, he saw a black silhouette in the window, the shutter banged, and the man was gone. Argand pulled himself to his feet, staggered to the tall rectangle of night sky, and then slipped as he trod on something hard and round. The resulting jar was as bad as anything he had yet suffered — it was with a shooting pain in his back that he at last got to the sill.

Palms heaved and rattled in the breeze from the sea, moonlight glowed on the expanse of ocean beyond and the light flickered at the end of the low blackness on the horizon that was Santa Prudencia. Below shadows moved swiftly amongst the tossing oleanders, across the lawns, came and went with the lamp from the hotel entrance and the glow from the street lights between the hotel and the sea. The drop was five metres, no more, no problem for an athlete who knew what he was doing — and his assailant had certainly been that.

Argand pulled in the shutters and fastened the window, then made his way carefully back to the light switch, still leaning on the furniture as he went, and holding his shaken, twisted back muscles. With the light he blinked, took in the scene he had expected. Everything in the room had been moved, turned over, taken apart. The search had been meticulous, working from the window inwards, and had reached the head of the bed by the door. One pillow slip had been removed, the other was still in place. All the drawers had been turned out, his clothes piled loosely in a corner, his grip and the document case turned upside down beside them. Nothing had been damaged, but everything had been touched.

Argand returned to the window. It had not been forced. Nor had the door. He guessed that entry had been through the door, probably with a pass key that the intruder had taken with him. He had opened the window and shutters to create the escape route he had actually used. All in all, a professional job, carried out by a man who knew exactly what he was doing. He had been dressed for the job too — heavy shoes but rubber-soled, a smooth sweater, light gloves, nylon stocking pulled over his face.

All this went through Argand's mind as he sat on the bed and waited for his breath to come back, his heart to stop pounding, the pain in his back to become bearable. Then, when he was ready, he stood up and began to set everything to rights, working just as methodically as the intruder he had disturbed. The man must have heard him coming, he reflected, the key perhaps, turned out the light just as he opened the door. . . .

He stooped to tuck in the bedclothes and as he did so his foot kicked something that rolled away under the bed. His back jarred again as he went down to see what it was. A marble, a glass marble, was that what he had trodden on on his way to the window? No. Not a marble. From the palm of his hand an eye looked up, unblinking. A glass eye.

X

CALLE Cervantes 8 turned out to be a small building in a side street not far from Avenida de Venezuela — but areas change quickly in style and prosperity in Las Guavas and there was nothing chic about Cervantes. Small blocks, many of them carrying the yoke and arrows of the Falange which signified that they had been built with government subsidies under Franco, alternated with warehouses, a small school, and the sort of small factories that exist on the ground floors in many city streets in Spain — turning out cheap furniture, metal fittings for doors and windows, potteries producing 'ethnic' plates and jugs for the tourists. Number eight had no janitor, and two small children played in the hallway.

Argand took the lift to the seventh floor, which was as far as it would go. He got out on to a small landing with four front doors. Three of them had tin sacred hearts, all of them had name-plates. None announced Salim Tumbal. A narrow staircase turned corners round the winding gear of the lift shaft and Argand followed it to the top. Two front doors now faced him, sharing the top step with no landing — *Atico Izquierda, Atico Derecha*. The door of *derecha* was ajar, with a Yale-type key in the keyhole. Above the bell a card had been pinned. Argand read: *Salim Tumbal Robertson, agente general*. Then the address. Argand rang the bell — it sounded a yard or so away, on the other side of the door.

A fly buzzed against the high sloping skylight above the stair-well behind Argand's head. He turned, watched it sink to the frame, then it buzzed again, began a zig-zag ascent of the glass. Beyond, a long way beyond, a cloud in the otherwise clear sky slowly shifted shape — a camel, then a weasel. Argand rang the bell again and, as if the button had activated it, the cased-in winding mechanism whirred and the lift descended. Perhaps, thought Argand, Salim has gone down to the tiny shop on the ground floor and is now on his way back up. He waited. The lift stopped. Then it whirred briefly, but made it only as far as the third or fourth floor. The fly started again and the cloud became a whale. Argand walked through the door.

It was not a large flat — two rooms, a kitchenette and a bathroom. A wide balcony with a high wall went round three sides. On the fourth the wall was even higher, fencing it off from next door. Inside the ceilings sloped with the roof. The first room was furnished with cheap modern stuff, a table, four chairs, a sofa. There was a hi-fi, and on the walls were two cheap hangings in machine-woven fabrics — one depicted the Taj Mahal, the other a Sultan surrounded by a harem of trousered girls. They had veils but their breasts were bare. A brass coffee set seemed to go with them. There were two framed photographs — one of the Rock of Gibraltar, the other of a British Army sergeant, smiling, holding a dusky baby.

The bedroom was smaller. Just a narrow bed, a chair, a wardrobe, a chest of drawers, and a pile of magazines like the one Salim had offered Argand on the plane. Salim himself was on the bed. He looked as if he had been dead for some hours.

Argand checked this first impression. The body was cold, the first stage of rigor mortis quite well advanced. The cause of death was obvious: he had been garrotted with picture wire — but inexpertly or at any rate inefficiently. Salim's face was swollen and suffused, the eyes popping, the blackened tongue protruded. Prolonged constriction of the windpipe had preceded dislocation of the vertebrae. There were also signs that his last hours had been unpleasant. Four burn marks overlapped and tracked up his cheek to the corner of his right eye. The bruising round the mouth had begun to grow out — yellowing until death cut short the healing process.

The body was clothed, much as it had been when Argand last saw it alive, there were still blood stains on the shirt, but he didn't feel at all sure that it had been clothed when it died. But this was not something he could be sure of without interfering more than he wanted to — throughout his investigation he was meticulous about leaving no sign that would indicate how thorough he had been. He went through the pockets and found nothing exceptional — money, residence permit, two more small keys, and two till receipts for small amounts, that was all.

Argand sat down on a chair in the living-room. For two minutes he just sat, staring at his thumbs, his mind numb, blank. He felt very tired, experiencing the remoteness of reality, and every inch of his body felt flaccid as well. He listened to his breathing as if even that was someone else's, and discovered that it was very shallow indeed, hardly more than moving the air up and down his windpipe. He took several deep breaths, expanding his rib-cage and pushing down with his diaphragm, and began to feel better.

He took a drink of water in the tiny kitchen and looked around. There was very little there — you could have made a cup of camomile tea, or coffee, but without milk; you could have drunk a quarter of a litre of DyC, Spanish whisky, and that was about it. There were no utensils, no means for cooking and eating even the simplest meal.

Argand walked back into the living-room. A voice, very deep but quiet, and menacing too, spoke to him from the bedroom.

"*Tengo una pistola. Siéntese a la mesa. No se vuelva Vd. Ponga las manos sobre la mesa.*"

Argand said, in English, that he did not speak Spanish.

"I have a gun. Sit at the table. Do not turn round. Put your hands on the table."

Argand did as he was told. His armpits were touched, his waistband, his jacket pockets. He caught a glimpse of a very large hand, very plump, and a whiff of expensive cologne. At last their owner came round in front of him, stood facing him, looking down at him over a small black pistol that was almost lost in the fist that held it. For a moment Argand was mesmerized by the tiny black muzzle, then he lifted his eyes and took in the man who stood behind it.

He was large, nearly two metres, and fat — but elegantly dressed in a beautifully cut suit made out of some almost silk-like wool with a slight sheen. The face, if it had smiled, would have been cherubic, the head was almost bald, what hair there was was silver and carefully cut.

"My name is Joachim. The boy in there is my stepson. Who are you?"

Argand answered, dwelling a little on the high rank he held in a European police force. He placed the gold-embossed, folded card that proved it on the table in front of him. Joachim held it flat with two spread fingers, then flipped it over. He put the tiny pistol beside it and sat down opposite Argand. His hand remained close to the pistol. He crossed his legs at the ankles and cleared his throat.

"I have been wanting to meet you for some time, Commissioner. For some forty-eight hours. Initially because I thought you would be able to tell me where a certain document case that my stepson was carrying had got to. Now, I have more pressing reasons." The huge head lifted a fraction, indicated with economy the bedroom beyond. "It seems to me that you may be able to throw light on how and at whose hands my stepson died."

Argand scarcely paid attention to this — he was suddenly

90

overcome with an intense excitement that stemmed from the realization that here was the lead he had been waiting for, here was the man who knew where the heroin had come from.

Joachim continued: "Sir, I am trying to deal plainly with you. I have made enquiries. I have contacts in Amsterdam and I have been able to speak to people who know Brabt, City and Province. It seems you have reputation, Commissioner. For honesty. That you are in bad odour with the authorities there, perhaps on account of that honesty. You have been seconded to advise IBORRAS on the American Base. In short, there is nothing at all to indicate that you have been investigating my concerns, and every reason to believe that our paths have crossed quite fortuitously. In the first instance, that is. But since that first chance moment your actions have brought nothing but harm to me and mine." He raised his voice a little, and through his own preoccupations Argand could not help being aware that there was menace here, even hate.

"Salim was carrying a package for me. For reasons I shall not now go into he exchanged the case he was carrying it in with a similar case — the one you were carrying. When he did this I am not sure. Perhaps on the plane, perhaps at Madrid airport. Subsequently he followed you with the aim of changing the cases back or at least of finding out what you had done with his. You were violent with him. The same evening he was arrested but not charged. He used his legal right to a telephone call to make contact with me, and I arranged his release through my lawyers, expecting he would come home." The gem dealer detected a response from Argand and he explained: "This was not Salim's home. He lived with his mother and me. He kept this place to entertain . . . women, when he felt the need. Let me conclude. He did not come home. Twelve hours after his release I find him here dead, and later, I find you hiding in the kitchen. You will understand why

91

I believe you must know more about his death than I."

Argand remained silent, waiting, hoping the gem dealer would say more. Joachim sighed, his fingers tapped the butt of the tiny pistol. It was black, shiny, put Argand in mind of certain shells, mussels perhaps.

"Come, sir. You are trying my patience. I have it in mind to bend you a little. I have channels, discreet, but they exist, ways of communicating with certain law enforcement agencies in Europe and the States. If I were to pass on the exact nature of the goods poor Salim was carrying, that those goods are still presumably in your possession . . . yes, I think you take my point. Your connection with Salim is already a matter of police record. With your presence here discovered at the side of his dead body, nothing less than a very full investigation of your activities would follow."

This time Argand was not able to restrain his reaction. Joachim's threat to expose him for being in possession of heroin so exactly matched his own idea of what lay behind the swapped cases that he twisted away towards the patio door, scarcely concerned when the gem dealer snatched up the pistol and levelled it at his body. He turned back.

"You cannot expose me without implicating youself. Your threat is hollow. As you say, I have a reputation. You too, I daresay, enjoy a reputation, of a different colour. It is childish of *you* to threaten *me* with the police."

Joachim put the pistol down on the table, drew out a large silk handkerchief, patted his cheeks and neck with it. Then he looked again at the gun, pushed it with a finger, and finally returned it to the inside pocket or holster it had come from. A smile hovered reluctantly in the corners of his mouth.

"It was not loaded," he said. "I carry it to frighten off muggers. Commissioner. We must both be more frank with each other than we have been. You think you know what I am up to. There is after

92

all a very good market for the contents of Salim's case. I am a trader. Well. You must believe me when I say that there is a lot more to all this than that. And believe me too when I say that I am no longer interested in recovering the case or its contents. My only concern now is to bring to book my stepson's murderers. Familial responsibility indicates that I should. There are other reasons. In the areas where I operate, it is not good that word should get around that the people who work for me can be . . . removed with impunity. So much for that. I may be more explicit if what you tell me indicates that I should be. Now. I believe that our interests can be made to coincide, though I am still not clear just where yours lie. If you could be more explicit I might help you. Meanwhile I reiterate. My concern is simply to uncover and bring to justice my poor stepson's murderers."

He paused, put his head on one side. His expression became quizzical. "That you have an interest is evident. You are a respected policeman. The Honest Commissioner. There is a world of inference in that sobriquet. Yet — let us beat about the bush no more — a case containing illicit wares comes into your possession and what do you do? You do not go to your colleagues. Apparently you hide it. Then, when you trap the man whom you know to have been carrying it, what happens? You beat him. Then, as a consequence perhaps? I don't know, he is arrested. If you would indicate what is behind all this, then, as I say, we may move to a position where we might be of assistance to each other."

The excitement returned and confused Argand as he searched around in his mind for the right way of moving to the next step. He sensed sincerity in Joachim's insistence that he wanted Salim's murderers brought to book — after all the gem dealer, smuggler, had indicated good reasons beyond the claims of mere justice. He pulled himself straight.

"You have not been frank with me. Not at all. But you have said

93

enough. I understood from the start that neither you, nor your stepson, nor whoever employed you were involved in trafficking in heroin, I understand why you say that you are not concerned with recovering it." He paused. Somewhat wildly his eyes took in again the sorry little room with its tawdry hangings and bazaar fittings, then returned to the broad expanse of Joachim's face. The gem dealer's eyebrows were raised, an expression of astonished curiosity was slowly forming, and this Argand found suddenly and deeply irritating — the impatience he had not yet learnt to control reasserted itself, and against his better judgement he pushed on. "You spoke of moving to a position where we might help each other. But you have not moved far enough. Tell me one thing, and I will see what I can do to help you. One thing."

"Well?"

"A few minutes ago you said you would not go into why the cases were swapped. But I *know* why they were. If we are to co-operate you must tell me — who employed you to plant heroin on me?"

Silence. The fly buzzed on the pane of glass beyond the still open door; traffic murmured below. Two sparrows suddenly swooped into the balcony, courting, the male fanning out its plumage, trailing its wing tips, then they were off again.

At last Joachim spoke, slowly shaking his huge head from side to side.

"Commissioner. No one employed me, or Salim, to plant heroin on you. That is the truth."

Excitement, anticipation evaporated; a sudden chill distilled gall and disgust in their place — much of it self-disgust that he had been ready to bargain with this crook. Argand picked up his embossed warrant card and pushed his way round the table, knocking one of the chairs sideways as he did.

Joachim watched him go and the expression of surprised dis-

94

belief remain fixed on his face. Perhaps it occurred to him then that the Honest Commissioner's actions really were irrational — the products of a disturbed mind.

Back in his room that night Argand felt worse than at any time since his discharge from Brabt State Hospital, the Psychiatric Wing. He was deeply confused and could not bring his mind to bear on anything for more than a moment for two. He could not eat and he suffered sudden and staggering changes of temperature. He feared that the intruder of the previous night might return and for that reason he did not take his medication until well after midnight by which time fantasies concerning the day's events had merged into waking nightmare — Joachim, Salim dead, the digger, spinning blue lights and police sirens, and the glass eye that he clenched in his fist underneath the pillow. Finally he succumbed and took the full dose.

In the first grey light he woke from his sedated sleep to an involuntary ejaculation accompanied by a warm, palpable vision of Françoise Brunot which became confused, in his dream, with the image of the girl on Salim's and Cortés' magazine. This time his self-disgust would have driven a man without his beliefs to thoughts of suicide — but his was a view of human nature that had its roots in a deeply Christian upbringing: no experience of sin, however degrading, in himself or in others, could ever surprise, let alone overwhelm him. However, cleaning himself up with cold water, he found himself wondering about the woman whose image had so shamefully disturbed him — he still did not know why it had been arranged that his case should come into her possession. She had turned away his questions. He would have to do better at a second attempt.

XI

ARGAND spent that morning at the IBOBRAS head office with Peters. They completed the *aide-mémoire* for the Governor and began to discuss in detail the layout of what would be the administrative area of the Base. Where he was professionally involved Argand usually contrived to overcome any presumably irrational feelings against his colleagues — he would hardly have made it to full Commissioner without this gift — and in this instance he found Peters receptive to his ideas, indeed respectful, and that was a help. Like most dedicated but lonely men Argand had a vein of vanity which, once you were aware of it, was touchingly easy to tap.

He explained his famous inside-out theory of planning for internal security: how buildings can be laid out, facilities installed, access roads stitched in so that a complex can be made proof against the effects of riot on one side and yet provide no secure area where a sit-in can be maintained or terrorists hole up. He sketched out rough diagrams on transparent film so they could be imposed over the site plans and "Hey, Jan, now that is *dynamic*, you're the greatest since Haussmann, I mean you really have grasped the *dialectics* of this situation," Peters exclaimed. Argand replied modestly that the concept was working very well in the new Arts Faculty at Brabt University.

Two girls in maroon dresses brought them coffee in red and gold cups. At IBOBRAS almost everything that could be was in a combination of red and gold.

"So your heroin-smuggling accomplice came to a bad end," said Peters, stretching out his legs, exposing thighs that made his light-weight trousers look like well-filled sausages. Argand flinched away, took his cup to the rose-tinted window. They were thirty floors high — across the bay he could see the ruined *vega* where the Base would be, the weirdly-shaped tufa hills, and finally the jagged crest of San Cristóbal. "Come on, Jan. Quit being so touchy. I don't mean it, you know I don't. But hell, I'm curious. No, but really."

Argand looked down. The height didn't bother him. Across the road from the entrance to the IBOBRAS building, pickets with banners against the Base had collected. Police in grey uniforms with black riot sticks watched them warily. If Pérez knew his job, and Argand was sure he did, there'd be a couple of his Panhard or GKN Sankey personnel carriers pushed up a nearby sidestreet.

He turned, aware suddenly of alarm, a warning signal, pricking in his diaphragm. His voice was level.

"Curious?"

"Sure. Come *on*. A police chief doesn't sit next to a heroin smuggler on a plane by accident. It's not a coincidence when a few days later he turns up in the guy's apartment and finds him dead. Hey, I *know* you're on the level as IS adviser to IBOBRAS and all that, but that doesn't mean you needn't be moonlighting. Doing a bit of drug law enforcement in your spare time. Is that it?"

"Not exactly."

"Not *exactly*?"

No sound. Just traffic below.

Argand sighed, put down his cup.

"You're right," he said. "Coincidences like that don't happen. I'll tell you the truth, as I told it to Colonel Pérez last night."

He explained in cold tones that he had powerful enemies in Brabt; that he believed that they had tried to frame him; that perhaps Salim had been killed so a line that might have led back to the originators of the plot would be cut off. Well, he would see. He had other avenues to explore; he wasn't without further resources.

"Yeah? And what are they, I wonder?"

Argand clutched the glass eye in his pocket and said nothing.

Peters stood up, placed himself two paces away from Argand. His breath was sour, like old yogurt.

"Did José Pérez believe you? Believe that stuff about enemies in Brabt?"

Argand peered at the thick spectacles, tried to make contact with the unblinking eyes beyond.

"I suppose so. Why not?"

"Sure as hell I don't." Peters turned away, set down his cup. "These guys who bumped off your Salim seem a pretty ugly bunch. You'd better know what you're up to. I mean, hell Commissioner, you're doing a great job here, I mean, *take care*, won't you?" He turned back, a big smile baring small yellowish teeth.

They were to have lunch, a barbecue, at Guzmán's finca.

"A working lunch they call it, but Spics really don't understand the concept. Anyway Colonel Javier de la Cerda will be there — he's to be OC Legion on the eighth, and you'll be able to advise him on escorting the digger. For the rest it'll be too much booze and indigestible meat."

They drove up in an IBOBRAS car, making a detour through the site. They stopped briefly to see how Argand's projections fitted into what was left of the actual landscape. Since they had been there last a new crop of sprayed slogans had appeared and work was almost at a standstill. Most of the labour force had anticipated the next day's general strike.

As they left the site the car was recognized and a stone clanged on its wing, chipping the red paint. Peters accelerated away, up into the tufa foothills.

"They're touchy at the moment because of the digger. But once that's sorted out labour'll come round. Organized labour anyway. They know their noses from their asses. After that it'll be separatists and anti-nuke freaks, and they don't amount to very much."

"Not the separatists?"

"Hell no. With the ongoing shortfall economywise they need metropolitan Spain. I can't see how a meaningful momentum towards greater independence can maintain a significant thrust."

He changed gear noisily, pulled round a convoy of three camels led by a donkey.

"Goddamn steam gears. Still, the situation is by no means static, and here we have to recognize that our own Project Achilles might just turn out to be the crypton factor. You know — we have a lot to learn from our friends in the ecological field. If you build a dam, alter a climate, drain a marsh you alter an eco-sphere, and it's the ecologists' job to make projections about just what those changes will be. Now Project Achilles is going to inject billions of dollars into the island economy and who knows what effect it'll have on the socio-political sphere? It's a thought, you know Jan; it's a thought."

He looked sidelong at Argand, but got no response. To tell the truth, Argand wasn't that interested in the finer points of Santa Caridad politics, was slightly irritated that Peters seemed to think he was — the way one is when an acquaintance keeps harping on a cultural lacuna in one's make-up.

The landscape changed again. The road took them over a pass and hills fell away to the ocean, but these hills were different. They supported deciduous woods and fields — some stubble, some parched grass. The soil too was brown, a pleasant relief after the blacks and slatey greys of the volcanic cinders. Peters explained: the mountains they had crossed were the highest on the island after San Cristóbal, and had protected the land beyond from the fall-out of successive eruptions. What they could see now were the oldest visible rocks on the island; it all indicated what it would have been like if only old San Cristóbal had kept his hat on.

It was the most favoured part of Santa Caridad, and Guzmán's finca was set like a pearl in its heart. They left the main road; an unmetalled but smooth enough track hairpinned up terraced slopes through cypresses and eucalyptus to a long low villa set into the hillside. They parked below it in a quadrangle formed by old stone barns. There were several vehicles there before them — a black Mercedes, two buses, an army staff car, and three or four more, all large and expensive. Clearly the barbecue was not for IBOBRAS advisers only.

They climbed a long flight of shallow stone stairs flanked with bougainvillaea, jasmine and a shrub covered with delicate blue star-shaped flowers, and so on to an open belvedere, a three-quarter circle set at the end of a long parterre that spread in front of the villa. Tables were set out, bottles and glasses gleamed on white napery, servants stood behind them. In a large corner, just behind the top of the stairs they had climbed, there were three wide stone troughs filled with white charcoal that glowed when the air breathed across it; more tables supported gridirons covered with slabs of steak, thick pork chops, sausages, and lumps of lamb or veal. Chefs in high hats threw handfuls of herbs on to the coals just as they arrived and set the first grills over the white aromatic smoke that billowed round them.

Peters took Argand's elbow. The American was panting from the brief climb and mopped sweat from his thick red neck.

"Nice pad, eh Jan? I mean it's a swell place. And the hunting's good too. If Franco did spend his honeymoon here then I reckon doña Carmen didn't get too much bothered. What do you say? A great guy with a hunting gun was the old Caudillo, bless his soul. Whisky or wine, Commissioner?"

Jan would have liked to have said neither. Cold water would have suited him well enough. The wine was dark, tasted heavy, fruity. He feared his headache would return. Peters took a tumbler of scotch poured over ice and then, to Argand's relief, padded away into the small crowd. Argand hung back and looked over them all.

There were thirty or forty people there, and at first glance they shared one unmistakable characteristic — all were well-to-do. The men, for the most part middle-aged or even elderly, were dressed in lightweight suits with expensive ties and shoes in fancy leathers; the women were coiffured, wore silks or very finely spun wools, diamonds flashed from tanned fingers, gold gleamed chunkily on thin wrists or lay across scrawny breast bones. Conversation was animated, and if the frequent outbursts of hearty laughter were a guide, genial, even witty. The breeze gusted and the smell of burning meat assaulted Argand's nostrils.

"Hallo there, Commissioner. You look as if one of us is a multiple murderer, but you're not quite sure who."

Jan turned, found he was looking into half-moon glasses and twinkling blue eyes.

"Hallo. Professor Shiner?"

"You remember. But of course it's your trade, one of your skills. You were looking very dismal just now — it must be that stuff you're drinking. Now let me get you a good dram, with water of course, they've some very good scotch here and the water is very soft, just the ticket."

Shiner took Argand by the elbow to one of the tables where he carefully chose a bottle from the selection of five or six that were there, poured a finger of whisky and added two of water. In fluent Spanish but still with the accents of the Athens of North Britain he told the waiter what he could do with his ice.

"There we are. That should make things a little rosier."

Argand sipped and nodded. "Well, I didn't expect to find you here," he said.

"Nor I you. Though why not? Our host has his fingers in many pies. No doubt he is building your Base; and he is certainly chairman of the Cabildo committee for the promotion of the works of Jorge Benítez, so half the Congress is here today. . . ." He took a passing canapé. "You should try these little sausages, they're local and quite delicious."

"And where is Señor Guzmán?"

"There, over there on those steps. By that urn thing with the geraniums in it. Tall, white-haired. I can introduce you if you like."

"No. no. I have met him."

Salvador Guzmán's silvery hair seemed to float above most of his neighbours, his head permanently cocked on one side and turned down a little as if to catch what smaller mortals were saying. Beside him stood Pérez, almost as large but more lugubrious than ever. However, he smiled slightly at Argand, half waved, and Argand raised a hand in return.

"Ah, of course you know son-in-law too, police chief Pérez. Guzmán has a fair bit of Scottish blood in him, via the Argentine. Campbell, I believe. That's his wife just speaking to him now — striking couple they make, eh? She's a nob — very Almanac de Gotha. Of course it all takes a bit of keeping up, this sort of thing. Now that's an interesting chappie, there, that one who has just joined them, the military gentleman. See? Scarred down one cheek and right hand gone? Javier de la Cerda. He was only a lad when that happened to him. Subaltern at the siege of Madrid in '38.

Colonel now, should be a general, but they say he got on the wrong side of the Caudillo, years ago."

"You seem to know them all."

"Well, I told you, I've been in the Benítez racket for twenty years. And he's big business now. The more the world reads old Benítez, in schools, universities, wherever Spanish is taught, the better it is for Santa Caridad, the better for people like Guzmán. And now I'm a prof I can help. I set syllabuses, prescribe set books, recommend editions. So of course, now they're bringing out the definitive complete works, printed here in Las Guavas, they have asked me to be on the editorial board. I think they want us to eat."

A queue was forming near the grills. Shiner and Argand joined it.

Argand, his mind never quite forgetting the existence of potential or actual enemies asked: "Is Dr Brunot here?"

Shiner turned back to him: "No, no. She won't come to functions like this. Poor girl, she's down town eating *sancocho* with the local Party officials. The beef is really quite good. Guzmán has the only beef herd on the islands, the rest comes in chilled from the mainland." He spoke brusquely to the chef, indicating which piece he wanted from the grill. Apparently the first offered had not been well enough done. "No need to take unnecessary risks of salmonella poisoning," he said cheerfully, then, "Oh damn and blast, here I say . . ."

His plate had been knocked so the steak had dropped on to his foot, marking his trouser leg on the way.

Argand looked down at the slab of charred meat, already dusty from the stone floor, then up at the man who had brushed past them. He was large, ugly too, his face impassive. Only a tiny pulse throbbed beneath one eye. The other seemed not quite to focus, was fixed, Argand thought, not on Shiner, who continued to

103

grumble while dabbing his clothes, but on some point far out in the distant Atlantic. He recognized Carlos, Guzmán's bastard and occasional chauffeur.

Still ignoring Shiner he now took Argand's arm.

"Please come with me," he said. "My father is waiting."

Argand made his excuses to the professor and dutifully followed Carlos up the steps and into the house.

Peters had been right. Little work was done at lunch which, for special guests, was served indoors at a long table in an oak-lined room. Guzmán sat at the head, in a throne-like chair, beneath what appeared to be the original of the picture of liberal separatists facing a firing squad in 1832. Oddly enough, his wife, at the other end, had Juan Carlos and Sofía above her, though this may have been to draw attention to an undoubted similarity in feature between her and the King. Between were Peters, Pérez's wife — who took after her father but had her mother's strong jaw — and eight or nine of the wealthy Spaniards Argand had noticed on his arrival. Pérez himself was absent — too busy with the bank raids and preparations for the general strike and demonstration to stay for lunch. Argand was put next to Javier de la Cerda whom he tried to engage in conversation about the role of the Legion on the eighth. De la Cerda knew French, but was brusque in his refusal to pursue the subject.

"I know my job, Commissioner, and my men know theirs. The ones that didn't got killed — or deserted — years ago."

Argand was disconcerted by this — for he could see no reason for his presence other than the one given by Peters. Never had he felt such a fish out of water. It occurred to him to wonder if de la Cerda wore an eyepatch because he'd lost a glass eye — and he smiled wryly at the thought of rolling on the floor with this elderly, disabled hidalgo.

He never did discover why he was there. The meal passed off in an atmosphere of nerveless formality which seemed to subdue even Peters. Argand was conscious that at intervals almost everyone at the table quizzed him and spoke to him — usually in French. He put this down to what usually passes for good manners amongst the upper classes when they have a stranger, an *odd* stranger in their midst. But it felt like scrutiny.

Only one incident interrupted the flow of the meal. After the main course — veal-like fillets done quite to Argand's liking — Cortés, the banker, came puffing in. The steps from the car-park had clearly been too much for him, but he was in a good mood, blowing out his cheeks, rubbing his hands together. A place was set for him next to Guzmán, he waived the earlier courses and fell on his steak as if he had been starved for weeks. He had been present during the bank raid where the shooting had taken place — naturally everyone wanted to hear the details.

At last it was over. Most of the Spanish guests were already gone — still gleaming and immaculate, not a hair out of place, not a speck of grease on their perfectly pressed clothes. Their large cars purred down the terraces, glinted through the cypresses and eucalyptus. Up on the parterre a courier was trying to gather the academics from the Benítezian Congress, shepherd them down the stairs to their buses. Most of the foreigners were drunk. Unlimited supplies of good whisky, drunk in the open air, had proved to be too much of a temptation. A Swede had been sick over the geraniums in one of the urns and two French structuralists were singing *Alouette, gentille alouette*, miming the words exaggeratedly. Argand was left, for a moment or two, on his own. He stood on the parterre in the litter of plates, potato skins in crumpled foil, half-eaten lumps of bread and chewed gristle, and looked down the terraces to a tiny shack far away beneath him.

Smoke leaked through a turf roof. He wondered, most uncharacteristically, how often the people who lived there ate meat. He remembered *sancocho* and shuddered.

"Well, there we are then," said a voice behind him. Shiner again. "Glad to see you alive and well. I imagine you lunched with the nobs — good was it?"

"All right, I suppose." It occurred to him to say he would have enjoyed himself better outside, but he looked again over the litter and decided not to. Then his eyes narrowed. "Why should I *not* be alive and well?"

Shiner pursed his lips in mock, slightly camp surprise at being taken seriously. "You were led away by Don Carlos. He has a reputation."

"Really?"

"Too silly of me to mention it. But he was pushed downstairs when he was a youngster. Some say by his half-sister, your friend Pérez's wife. Some say by his step-mother. Probably just fell. Anyway he's never been quite right in the head since. Prone to violence and so on."

The structuralists went by. *Un ami à droite, un ami à gauche, vive la compagnie,* was now their song.

"Oh dear," said Shiner. "Oh well. We are to have coffee at a restaurant as near to the top of San Cristóbal as one is now allowed to get. That may sober them. And then on to the golf club. It used to be run by my fellow countrymen — Scots I mean, shippers from the port — but I gather the Japanese have taken over. *Ah fugaces!* One tries to maintain standards, it's all one can do, but . . ." He shrugged, smiled, shook Argand's hand. The gesture was oddly impulsive. Perhaps after all, he too had had a dram or two too many.

Peters drove back in silence, complained of a headache. As he dropped Argand at the hotel entrance Trencher came out. A

106

porter was packing his suitcases into a taxi.

"Local chappie came up with the chinks after all," he said on the steps, also taking Argand's hand. His breath smelt of gin. So much physical contact with his fellowmen in one day was becoming worse than distasteful, but Argand managed to keep back the scowl he felt coming.

"So you're off then?"

"Yes. All signed and sealed. Shipping agent will handle the actual transfer. No need for me now, so it's back to dear ol' Blighty. Shouldn't wonder if I don't get the Queen's Award for Exports at this rate. Well, cheerio old chap. Keep in touch, won't you?"

At last he let go of Argand's hand, gave him a pat on the shoulder and swayed down into the taxi. His hand luggage clinked as he handed it in.

"Don't forget," he called, "honey in your scotch at night," he tapped his nose with his skeletal finger. "Always does the trick."

His departure was the best news Argand had had all day.

XII

THE general strike was even more complete than expected. When at last a taxi was found for him, Argand discovered that the streets were almost empty, the shops closed. Small groups gathered at corners, and a van with a loudspeaker on top went by scattering leaflets. It was almost the only moving vehicle he saw.

At the police headquarters confusion reigned, panic even. Argand was kept waiting at the desk until a French-speaking officer could be found. Then it was explained that Pérez was in the screening-room and that Argand should join him there.

He was taken to the basement, to a small converted cellar. It was full and he had to stand at the back. The air was dense with tobacco smoke, his eyes began to run, and he could not see Pérez. He had almost decided to leave when the large TV screen at the end of the room glowed, the lights dimmed, and what appeared caught and held him. It did not matter that he could not understand what was being said.

He was looking from above, through a distorting wide-angle lens, at the hall of the bank where he had changed his travellers' cheques. He recalled the spherical camera with its four lenses.

The raiders were already moving down the hall towards the *caja*. In front of them came a policeman with his hands resting awkwardly on his white helmet. He had been disarmed. Otherwise it all looked much as it had done when the security men had called to collect specie and notes. Only the uniforms were different, and the arms. The raiders wore black berets, nylon masks, blotched

combat fatigues and were armed with Armalites and heavy auto-
matics, all except the apparent leader who had a Heckler and Koch
machine pistol.

The raid progressed. Even with frequent interruptions and re-
runs of the tape — apparently the audience had been gathered to
see if anyone could spot a feature which might help to identify the
raiders — Argand's curiosity was aroused by the way that almost
exactly the same routine was followed now as had been when he
was there in person.

The banker, Enrique Cortés, appeared on picture, produced the
plastic cards which activated the electronic locking mechanisms.
Then in the same brisk but unflustered way as before the doors
were swung back, the low steel trolley appeared, and the cashier
began to load it.

Then, suddenly, it went wrong.

For some reason the gangster with the Heckler and Koch came
round the trolley, just as the last bag was being placed on it, and
cut the corner so fine that he tripped over it. One of the cashiers
reacted — whether he was really attempting to interfere or
whether the gangster's stumble provoked an involuntary reaction,
was not clear — at all events the machine-pistol fired, a prolonged
burst at point-blank range. Ten rounds in six seconds and there
was the cashier, arms and face still writhing and grimacing while
blood spilled out of his middle as if from a ruptured pipe; there was
the gangster, head weaving from side to side as if trying to locate
and stamp out any further threat; and there was Cortés, his head
showing round the steel desk he had thrown himself behind and
mouthing some word, again and again.

The nastiness of it all was heightened rather than otherwise by
the distorting lens and the silence. Argand wondered why there
was no sound. There should have been.

There was not much else to see. The trolley was quickly

trundled down the hall, the gangster with the machine-pistol took up the rear, walking backwards and occasionally still stumbling, then they were beyond the range of the camera. There was a brief glimpse of terrified customers — an elderly woman was having hysterics — and the tape flickered to its close. The lights came on.

Those who had cigarettes put them out, those who did not lit up. Argand wondered if he might be sick. Pérez stood up, large and melancholy like a camel, and most stopped talking. He spoke quietly, incisively, giving orders, offering advice and reprimand. He concluded: *"Señores, nada más,"* and squeezed his way through to the door.

"Commissioner. You found me then." He put a hand on Argand's shoulder. "We're in a hurry, but we can talk as we go."

As they climbed to the first floor and Pérez's office Argand reflected sympathetically that Pérez looked exhausted. He remembered similar periods of crisis he himself had suffered: one week in February three years before a gang of South Moluccans had hijacked a school bus — they had not realized that they had crossed the border and that the children were Brabanter not Dutch — and on the same day a train carrying nuclear waste had been derailed in a Brabt suburb. Over ten thousand people had had to be evacuated.

Pérez's office was large and years ago had been impressive. Now it needed redecoration; the veneer on the modern desk had begun to lift, the soft imitation leather on the chairs had grown brittle and was cracking. Large windows looked on to a yard that was equally drab. In concrete plant-holders cacti went brown and geraniums grew long and etiolated. Police in riot gear were spilling out of a door and lining up.

Pérez coped with his phones, issued more instructions, received reports. Then he too lit a cigarette which he put in a stubby yellow holder. It was the first time Argand had seen him smoke.

110

"They're bringing a car to take us to the port. Well. What did you think of that?"

"Of what?"

"Of the film. Video-tape."

"It was a nasty business."

"Of course. But . . . was there anything about it that struck you? Anything we might have missed?"

This was oddly put. It was not a question that could be answered without a digest of all that Pérez and his experts had learnt from the tape — Argand frowned, looked out of the window. In the yard the police with visored helmets, shields, padded uniforms, batons were climbing into a Panhard armoured personnel carrier.

"I mean . . . in a general way. You have seen it once. It was about the tenth time I have seen it. I may now have lost some only half-grasped first impression; or perhaps your routines in Brabt are different and you may have noticed some oddity I have missed."

"Was that the only shooting?"

"Thank God — yes."

Argand bit his thumb. "There was no sound."

"No. A failure in the recording device. Are you suggesting a connection between the loss of sound and the shooting?"

Argand shrugged. He felt needled a little, still wondered what Pérez was getting at. He began to wish he had not seen the tape.

"Nothing else?"

"I should have liked to know what Señor Cortés was shouting."

"*Dios*, what a question! I wouldn't ask the poor man unless I thought it was important. What does one shout at such times? Whatever it is, inevitably one makes a fool of oneself. Anything else?"

"It would be interesting to know why the killer was so clumsy."

"Poof. We'll ask him when we catch him."

Argand's eyebrows rose into semicircles. Outside the Panhard engine began to rev. The GKN Sankey, Rolls-Royce version is quieter, he thought. He said: "I was intrigued to see how what happened followed so exactly the routine used by the security guards when I was in the same bank the other day."

Again the hand on the shoulder.

"What a professional you are! We had noticed the similarity too. No doubt the raiders studied the procedure."

He went on to tell Argand how the Renault vans had been hired and ditched, that the same routine but without casualties had been followed in the other two banks, that the total haul amounted to thirty million pesetas.

"Look," he said, "these have been distributed in the streets."

He handed Argand a sheet of cheap paper. As he took it he felt a sense of relaxation, as though now they were off the subject of the video-tape things would go more easily. Dimly he wondered why this should be so, and the thought dissolved.

The paper was still gritty from the sidewalk where it had been picked up. The material on it had been duplicated with Gestetner or Roneo equipment including a scanner. There was a picture of a bereted soldier waving a Heckler and Koch. The top line of Letraset capitals read: FUERZA MILITAR PARA LA LIBERACION DE LAS VIRTUDES M — L IV.

Argand said: "M — L means Marxist-Leninist and the IV means that they support the Fourth International." This time the echo in his unsettled mind was of Brunot and his humiliating dream of her in which her nipples had been large and brown, like the girl's on the magazine cover. His nails dug into his palms.

Pérez did not notice his distress.

"That's right. The rest claims they were responsible for the raids, that the money will be used to finance opposition to the Base and so on. I am sure you are familiar with the sort of thing."

"Who are they?"

"They're new. We think they are a military wing of the *Junta*

112

Popular. It has no funds worth speaking of. Anyway, last night we arrested their leaders, closed their offices, and impounded their files. And so we'll get enough on them to keep *them* under lock and key until the digger is on the site."

"It will be seen as provocation today."

"But today we're backing down."

The telephone buzzed. Pérez spoke, flicked switches, spoke again. Then: "That was my transport officer. He reckons we won't get through the crowd, so we'll have to use a chopper." Suddenly he smiled: "Well — now I must forget about the bank raids. The officers in charge are competent enough. Let's deal with this strike, shall we?"

Again Argand experienced the feeling he had had at Guzmán's lunch party: that beneath a semblance of good manners he had been scrutinized, tested. He presumed wryly that once again he had passed; he wished only he knew *what*.

As they were waiting for the helicopter on the roof Argand said: "Are you any further on with the murder of Salim Robertson?"

"Not really. We're not even absolutely sure any more of the cause of death. There were other less immediately obvious injuries and, well, the wire round his neck was not tight enough to have killed him on its own." Pérez had his eyes on three Sikorskys which were cruising a mile or so away over the port. One now tipped and swung out of the trajectory it had been on, began to clatter across the air towards them. "Actually there were electrode burns on his testicles. They must have been amateurs. There's no need to leave burns."

Argand thought he had his voice under control, but it fluked up on the first word. "Don't you . . . don't you have any idea who is behind all this?"

"No. As I said to you the other . . . Wait. I'll tell you inside."

What had been the size of an insect was now monstrous. It swooped towards them, hovered above them. The clatter was deafening, mind-blowing. Argand almost forgot, or relinquished the pressing reason he had for discovering who Salim's murderers were. The turbulence caught at their jackets and ties, Argand almost lost his hat. They ran across the flat roof and a strong arm helped them in. The hatch was closed, the noise was less unbearable, and with a sickening lurch the helicopter lifted up and away.

"Are you all right? I should have asked if you minded these things. Some people do . . . we'll be down in a minute."

"I'm all right. Salim . . ."

"Nothing more to say. He was a crook. His stepfather too. Free port. Usually we find them in the harbour. Never get to the bottom of such cases. Doesn't bother me unless some innocent is involved. *Hostia*, look at that. Well, don't if you'd rather not."

"Helicopter flight doesn't frighten me."

Argand looked out of the window, if only to conceal his mortification at being brushed off. Pérez leant forward, shouted to the pilot — the Sikorsky tipped again and the streets, quays and promenade floated up towards them. People, densely packed, filled every inch of space for hundreds of metres around the entrance to the port. Banners waved and here and there groups were obviously chanting — right fists clenched above their heads, flexing rhythmically, following cheer leaders.

In front of the harbour entrance three lines of police in full riot gear crouched behind portable barricades. Behind them were the armoured personnel carriers, ten GKN Sankeys and five Panhards. As far as they could see, in the fleeting moments they had, the confrontation was so far peaceful — the front rank of demonstrators keeping a narrow no-man's land between themselves and the barricades.

"What do you think of that?"

114

Argand grimaced. "There is not enough movement. Not enough flow."

Pérez pouted. "I know. But there are far more than we expected. It was meant to be a march. Avenida de Portugal, past the port, Avenida de Venezuela, and disperse at the roundabout, the plaza."

Argand thought: it was a bad mistake to lock up the leaders of the Junta. He would have called them out of the mob, threatened them, made promises, he would have endeavoured to weaken the mob's collective will by cajoling its leaders into giving contradictory orders. As usual his professional self had taken command. For the time being Salim was forgotten.

The radio crackled and they swung across the front, chasing their own shadow over the yacht club, the marina with its smart boats bouncing in the swell, out over the roads where a giant tanker waited off the refinery and an elegant square-rigged three master was dropping the pilot before standing off in the wake of Colombus. Then the quays were beneath them again, and, very close, so it seemed they would graze its roofs, exhaust pipes, chains, gantries and catwalks, the digger itself. Their turbulence scattered the black haze of diesel fumes that hung above it and then they were down, the clatter slowed, the motor throttled back, the long arms sank into relaxed parabolas and swung into stillness. Argand followed Pérez on to the quay.

Peters was there to meet them and together they moved off to the port entrance where a Saviem S95 command vehicle was parked amongst the others. As they climbed in a lieutenant spoke rapidly and with fear in his voice.

Pérez interpreted: "They have the Governor on the radio. He wants to mobilize the garrison. What do you think?"

"What would that mean?"

"Activity up at the barracks. Enough to be noticed."

115

"I should say no. You want to avoid any action that seems provocative."

"I'll tell him that."

Pérez took the handset, spoke briskly, though respectfully. Argand and Peters made themselves as comfortable as they could at the driver's end of the Saviem. Although surprisingly roomy — it had an extended chassis and was as long as a bus — it was already manned with four communications officers, the driver, and the lieutenant who had welcomed Pérez. At the rear there were switchboards, display maps and CCTV consoles. Everything vibrated, and none too gently, with the steady rumble of the rear-mounted engine, now functioning as a generator.

Standing up, Peters and Argand had a wide view of what lay in front. In the immediate foreground were the impedimenta of the security forces — spare moveable barriers, EARP projectors capable of laying down a barrage of gas and smoke bombs, another radio and telephone unit. Beyond came first the officers, then the backs of the three ranks of riot police with the visors of their riot shields and the tips of their batons projecting above their helmets. Finally the mob itself: a sea of wild faces, tousled hair, waving jerking fists and arms, and, above them, tossing and twisting as if in a gale, the banners.

NO A LA BASE. YANQUIS GO HOME. EL IMPERIALISMO DE CARTER = FASCISMO = CATASTROFE NUCLEAR. DISUASIVA — SI PRIMER GOLPE — NO.

"You see that banner, the big one," Peters asked. "Do you know what that says?"

" 'Deterrent yes, First Strike no'," said Argand. "Is that right?"

"That's right. Your Spanish is coming along fine. I tell you, that one worries me."

"Why?"

"It's all in here." Peters lifted up a paper that had been tucked

116

under his arm. The red masthead said *El Obrero Virtuoso* with a hammer and sickle in the corner. Beneath, a headline in one-inch letters repeated the slogan on the banner. Peters unfolded it and took out three centre folds.

"Special supplement," he said, and went on, translating, summarizing. "Why the Base will mean nothing less than the total destruction of Santa Caridad. We live with the fear that San Cristóbal may not be extinct, may blow its head off without warning as did Peña de Santa Cruz on Santa Templanza in 1874. But that does not mean we should also live in the certain knowledge that we will be the first victims of the nuclear holocaust when it comes. . . ." He folded the paper up and spoke directly to Argand. "They've gotten hold of a set of plans and stages of the Base, not classified, but taken together sensitive enough. And they've done their homework, give them credit for that. Out of it all they've worked out that the Base need not be just so defensive, *shield*-like, as our PR has been saying. You know what I mean?"

"The counterforce syndrome."

"Yeah," Peters looked up. His small eyes were cold, narrowed behind his glasses. "You know about that too."

"I know you are developing a weapons system that will be capable of knocking out not only the Russian centres of population following a nuclear attack on you, but of pre-empting a Russian attack by knocking out simultaneously all their rocket silos and submarines. You said as much the other day."

"That's it," Peters looked away. "Commissioner, where do you think this, all this," he tapped the newspaper, "came from?"

Argand felt heat rise in his face. He too looked out of the window.

Peters went on: "Do you suppose . . ." But before he could press further Pérez interrupted from the other end of the vehicle.

"Commissioner. Could you come up here a moment?"

117

Faster than was necessary Argand joined him.

"We've worked out our next step. We'd like your opinion."

They were going to start up the digger and move it down the quay. When the reaction from the mob reached a dangerous intensity they would halt it, if necessary move it back to where it now was. A little later the Governor would announce on the local radio and television that the digger was to stay put, that union leaders and other spokesmen for the population were to meet him immediately to draw up an agenda for detailed talks on the whole situation, and that no further work would be done on the site pending the outcome of these talks. People in the crowd carrying transistors would be asked to turn up the volume so everyone could hear the Governor's message, which would be repeated until the situation was back to normal.

Meanwhile Pérez's reserves, one thousand of them, were being bussed down the other side of the isthmus to assemble at the far end of Avenida de Portugal. When they were deployed they would move in behind the mob and begin to exert steady pressure to get the crowd moving away from the port entrance and up Avenida de Venezuela.

Once the crowd began to move the five hundred regulars in front of them would deliver a baton charge under cover of a gas bomb barrage, and Pérez hoped that would be it.

Argand listened, pored over the maps, chewed his lip, then straightened, hands on his hips.

"I don't think the baton charge will be necessary," he said. "I think you'll find that bit about stopping work on the site will do the trick. The backbone of that mob is organized labour who want the work the digger is depriving them of. They'll want these talks out of the way as soon as possible if they're going to be out of work while they're on. That was good thinking on your part. No. I don't think you're going to need a baton charge."

Pérez shrugged. "I'm afraid it's expected. The Governor expects

118

it. Every businessman and landowner on the island expects it. The media. We have mainland TV here. They want exciting film to send back. And for all I know, *they*," he gestured at the mob, "expect it too."

They made final adjustments to the plan. Messages were radioed out, answers came in. CCTV cameras were turned on the mob and the monitors in the command vehicle filled the small space with their sub-aquatic glow. Sergeants from the riot police were brought in to identify and mark the ringleaders. These would be singled out as the targets for signal pistols loaded with heavy rubber cylinders twenty centimetres long. Pérez explained that these would hit the ground in front of the ringleaders, the cylinders would bounce, and turning viciously hit their targets between knees and chest, hopefully in the crutch. "I've seen film of them being used in Northern Ireland," he said. "This is our first chance to try them out here."

On the quay the digger began to move. The cloud of black smoke above it thickened, the helicopters buzzed in more closely. Argand found Peters at his shoulder again, caught the tang of the American's sour breath. He was still holding *El Obrero Virtuoso*.

"You know Jan, this sure as hell fits those handouts we gave you in Brabt, you know — the briefing material."

"You know I lost my case at Barajas airport."

"Sure. I remember. And we checked it out. The passenger who returned it to the airline is a woman, some academic here for a literary conference. I don't think she's behind it."

"No?" Argand turned away. Not for the first time he wondered what Peters was concealing behind what appeared to be stupidity.

Two hundred metres away, down the quay, the giant digger picked up speed. Its four engines almost drowned out the noise of the mob, though that too began to rise to an orchestrated crescendo.

119

XIII

AGAIN the intruder at the Casa de Colón; again the secretary who could speak French was brought down from her office upstairs.

"I am sorry M'sieur, the final session of the day ended ten minutes ago. But if M'sieur is in a hurry to see a *congresista*, if it is important he may catch the person at the Museo de Santa Caridad . . . yes, M'sieur, the entire *Congreso*, a special guided tour. Go up to the Plaza Mayor, pass in front of the cathedral and on the corner opposite the far end of the church, there the museum finds itself . . . *de nada, Señor, adiós*."

Argand stepped briskly back into the narrow street and was grimly amused at the antics of the three men who were following him. Not only were they attempting to conceal from him what they were, but from each other too. Since, because of the strike, there was no one else in sight and all the shops and cafés were closed, they achieved only absurdity. Two turned to each other and simultaneously asked each other for a light; the third, no more than a boy really and the nearest, lost himself in rapt contemplation of the very short and boldly lettered inscription on the door-post.

As he walked up the narrow winding pavement towards the square, Argand reflected that the two who had been forced to snap cigarette lighters in each other's faces were almost certainly policemen, which was interesting, not to say puzzling, and should have been worrying — but worry was at that moment beyond Argand. A sudden burst of angry irritability at the end of the demonstration

(Argand never liked to see heads broken) had turned Pérez pale and drawn an exclamation from Peters, and had been a warning. He had dosed himself with tranquillizers and was now experiencing a brief euphoria.

He could think of good reasons why Pérez should put a man behind him: he was surely in some danger, however vague, since Salim's murder. But it was odd that there should be two, and two who had clearly been unaware of each other's existence, at least when Argand left police headquarters where he had been dropped by helicopter half an hour ago.

The third was not a policeman. He was a young lad, about fourteen, dark-skinned but not so dark as to be definitely not European, dressed in a denim top, patched jeans and broken down bumpers. It was possible, just, that the two policemen had not spotted him, for in many ways he was the most skilful of the three.

For instance, as he paused now and looked up at the cathedral spires — the dark brown, almost black stone was really not at all attractive — he could spot the policemen but the youth had disappeared. A blank space on the wall of the cathedral had been sprayed — NO A LA MISA TRIDENTINA.

At the other end of the façade a small group hung outside a doorway opposite — even at this distance they looked like academics, their chatter alone gave them away. Argand quickened his pace; with luck he might filter into the museum with them, and if it was a special guided tour and the museum was shut to the general public then this ridiculous procession of tails might be excluded.

The plan worked perfectly. Except that when he got in amongst the last seven or eight *congresistas* — as he expected they ignored him, took him for granted — he found the youth there before him, tugging at coat sleeves, grubby hand out: "*pesetas para sancocho, pesetas para sancocho,*" he was whining. An appeal that had no

121

expectations beyond a helping of inedible fish stew was clearly a touching one — he was doing well. He even had the nerve to try it on Argand: big brown eyes — was there a hint of mockery in them? — the practised tug — *"pesetas para sancocho."*

Inside the hundred or so *congresistas* were milling slowly through a succession of rooms too small to hold more than a third of them at a time. For the most part they ignored the exhibits and continued to ignore Argand too, were clearly still deeply involved with whatever had been the subject of the day's concluding paper. In truth the exhibits were not that interesting, consisting, at this level, of small fossils and large diagrams — the usual flow-charts of geology and evolution. Argand looked over the thirty or so people around him as methodically as he could, found no sign of Brunot, and set about trying to insinuate himself further up the crowd.

This was not easy: the *congresistas* showed a tendency to stop as soon as any obstruction got in their way — the result was a series of jams that it was difficult to squeeze through without drawing attention to oneself; and Argand now realized that they were all wearing name-flashes with their photos in colour on their lapels or bosoms, and he of course was not. It occurred to him at this point that he was acting in a way that was mildly irresponsible — certainly irresponsible by his standards. He wondered: had he overdosed himself, taken the pills twice?

They passed into a larger room which turned out to be the bottom of a well that extended to three more floors before reaching a skylight; each landing was fenced with a delicate wood and cast-iron balustrade, and walled with glazed cabinets. Slowly, very slowly, like high altitude climbers in thin air, they ascended. The fossils grew, became very large, and then smaller again. Artefacts appeared — or at any rate chips of stone that the labels claimed were artefacts — and then, more convincingly, shards of pottery, shreds of material, beads, and, at last, a gold coin. Still no Brunot.

They climbed again. A glassed-in coffin-like chest turned out to be just that — a bundle of brown bones nestled up against hard clay; eye sockets gawped darkly up at the scarcely more perceiving faces that peered in. Argand in his turn could not suppress a shudder; almost involuntarily he straightened, craned over the heads around him and momentarily fancied that every cabinet in the rooms that led off this, the last landing, housed nothing but footballs. In fact they were skulls. Thousands and thousands of skulls, three rooms full of skulls and nothing else at all.

He wondered why.

Each cabinet was labelled, but with figures, dates, names — perhaps place-names — only one word recurred again and again. Cro-Magnon. Cro-Magnon. Cro-Magnon.

Argand's recollections, distorted and rusty though they were, reminded him that Cro-Magnon man was a sub-species of *homo sapiens*, inhabiting certain areas in the extreme west of Europe; he painted rather well: Altamira, Lascaux; was generally thought to be a civilized, decent sort of chap amongst more barbarous cousins, possibly (though Argand would have been the last to admit this) because he, *she*, organized her society on matriarchal lines. But when? Ten millennia ago? Twenty? A hundred? He had no idea.

"We seem destined to meet in the unlikeliest places, Commissioner . . . ."

Quick, before he asks me what I am doing here.

"Professor. Perhaps you can tell me why all these skulls are here."

What professor can resist an opportunity for pedagogy?

His half-moon glasses twinkled up at Argand: "This," he said, "is the only museum of its kind in the world. I quote the tourist brochures. A comprehensive collection of Cro-Magnon skulls and artefacts. Actually very few artefacts, but a lot of skulls. Why? I will tell you. When the *conquistadores* arrived here — Santa Caridad was the first place to be blest in this way — they found Los Ponchos. Los Ponchos were heathen, naked, fun-loving, lost souls and received the usual come-uppance of such people. Rather quickly. Three hundred and fifty years later the Enlightenment followed the *conquistadores*. Rather late . . ." It occurred to Argand that Shiner too was high — on alcohol, or knowledge? ". . . and Los Ponchos were identified, unmistakably, their *remains* were identified as our old friend Cro-Magnon Man. And Woman. Now it is generally believed that Cro-Magnon was absorbed into other European races a very long time ago — though some say the Basques are Cro-Magnons — it was therefore very important that something should be made of this place, the last on earth where he lived undiluted. A sort of anthropological Galapagos . . ." This was lost on Argand. ". . . so naturally Hispanic pride dictated that he, she, should be resurrected, his civilization re-discovered, his artefacts exhumed. What a gift to our knowledge of early man! Unfortunately . . . all that remained were a lot of skulls. It's sadly significant that they are on the whole contemporaneous, and many are, well, broken."

Argand's euphoria was leaking away.

"It is as if," Shiner went on, and his mood too seemed to be changing, his tone suddenly cold, his articulation yet more precise, "the pits of Auschwitz were to be opened in four hundred years time and the skulls put on display — to demonstrate the achievements of European Jewry. Well, that's probably what will happen. Actually I was there when the graves were closed. At Auschwitz, I mean. Are you looking for Dr Brunot?"

"Yes."

"She isn't here. She's been once and does not care to return. I find it salutary to do so."

Argand turned away, pushing against the flow towards the stairs.

"But my dear chap. If it's urgent, come up. Come with us in our bus, up to the *Residencia Universitaria*, I mean. No one will mind. In fact hers is the room next to mine."

XIV

"*PASE*. Come in. Good gracious. You are the last person I was expecting."

"If it's inconvenient to see me now . . ."

"No. Not inconvenient, but I'm not sure if I *want* to see you."

Françoise Brunot was sitting at a desk beneath her window. In front of her were books, papers, a small typewriter. Between her and the door where Argand waited, hat in hand, two twin beds — both made. The room was barely furnished and more spartan than Argand had expected with only one small rug on the terrazo floor, two chairs both wooden and upright, and a small chest of drawers. On her table she had a vase of full-blown roses. Through the open windows and patio door Argand could see a long balcony, palm trees, and hills rising to the broken cone of San Cristóbal. A soft evening light was over everything, with mist rising between the lower hills.

"I think you ought to see me."

"*Ought*? What do you mean, Commissioner?" She tossed her head, and put aside the book she had been reading, marking the place carefully.

He went right in, went close enough to the table to drop *El Obrero Virtuoso* on it.

"Have you seen this?"

Colour rose in her cheeks.

"Yes. I have."

"Then I think you'll know why I'm here. The source for the

supplement inside that was the documents that were in my case. That's so, isn't it? Isn't it?"

She stood up. She was dressed in a wrap only which she now pulled more closely round her, retying the belt beneath her breasts. She was in a rising temper and Argand felt a tremor of discomfort. He was not at his best in scenes with women, and it was becoming clear that there was going to be a scene. And he was conscious too of how he was attracted by her.

"Commissioner, I will not be hectored by you. Nor will I deny that much of that article is based on photocopies of the material that I found in your case. And it was I who passed them on to the *Junta Popular Contra la Base*, and they passed them on to the paper. I don't see why that means I ought to see you."

"Because what you did was illegal. Because it is in my power to hand you over to the police."

Again she tossed her head. "Well do. Please do. Meanwhile kindly go and let me get on with my work."

He glanced down at her papers. One of the books was a small paperback. The title, *The Civil War in France*, was printed in red over the bearded, shaggy face with the giant forehead of the man Argand thought of as the evil genius of the times, the satan at whose door most of what was wrong with things could be laid. He shuddered, looked back into her dark eyes beneath thick unplucked brows.

"Why did you do it?" He spoke softly now, but no less urgently. "Why did you give those documents to those people?"

"I should have thought that was obvious enough. The Base is a disaster for Santa Caridad, Las Virtudes, and all the people who live here. It will bring a spurious and short-lived boom, but after that it will condemn the island to continuing and increasing poverty — mainly because the only solutions to the economic disease that afflicts this place are radical ones, and the Americans

127

will never allow them to be put into effect here once they have their Base. It will introduce a permanent garrison of foreigners that will amount virtually to an occupation. It will mean prostitution and a host of other evils. No. You asked me. Let me finish. Most important of all, the Americans are, as those documents — correctly interpreted — show, developing first strike capacity and this Base will be a very important part in that strategy. And first strike capacity is lunacy. It makes nuclear war a virtual certainty: for once one side has first strike capacity it will use it, use it when the other side seems close to achieving parity, if not before. Otherwise what is the point of having it? So, I knew it was my duty, as soon as I saw what was in your case, to pass it on where I thought it would do most good."

"Dr Brunot. I don't believe you. I don't believe that is why you passed those documents on to the Junta."

"Commissioner . . ."

But before she could go further there was another knock on the door.

"*Pase. Ah, Jorge, ya has venido. Te esperaba ¿sabes?*"

In the doorway stood a young man in a white shirt and black trousers. His hair was very dark, curly and glossy. White teeth glowed in a broad, open smile, which faded as he took in Argand.

"*Ay, perdone señora. No sabía que estaba . . .*"

"*No, No te marches Jorge. ¡Anda hombre! No te preocupes. Que sigas te digo.*"

"*¿Está segura?*"

"*Segurísima.*"

"*Muy bien señora. Muchas gracias.*"

"*De nada Jorge, de nada.*"

She gave him a wide open smile and the young man responded with a grin even broader than before, came right in, but then turned through the inner door into what Argand assumed was the bathroom.

Argand felt cold sweat breaking on his forehead, the sudden dryness in his throat, the tingling behind his eyelids.

"Commissioner. You were just saying, I think, that I am a liar."

"Yes. Yes, just that." And a whore too. The words were on the tip of his tongue, bursting to escape. "You were told to do it, perhaps paid, perhaps blackmailed into it, but however it was, you were *told* to pass on my documents to the Junta. Perhaps too you were told to take my case in the first place. I don't know. But I'm going to find out, I'm going to persuade you . . ."

Water exploded into the metal bath on the other side of the thin party wall and then settled into a steady roar. Jorge was taking a shower.

". . . and I'm going to make you tell me who told you to do these things."

"You're not going to make me do anything. You haven't got your bully boys about you now, you can't have me taken into a street doorway and battered with riot sticks until I bleed . . ."

Argand made an irritated gesture of dismissal.

"Not like that at all. Dr Brunot, you are a lecturer at Brabt University. The education of the young is in your care. Yet you are a Marxist; and your morals . . ."

"You think you can invoke Section 183 against me. Well, if you do the students will close the University until you withdraw."

Jorge burst into song: "*Poblador compañero poblador . . .*"

Argand raised his voice. "Or perhaps until the case is proved in open court and the public can see it was justly laid."

Por los hijos, por la patria y el hogar
Ahora la historia es para ti
Poblador compañero poblador . . .

"Can't you tell him to be quiet?"

"Certainly not."

"Then perhaps we can go somewhere else."

"On the balcony if you like."

He followed her out. Her room was set above what must have been a built-on extension of the original building — the consequence was that her balcony was deep, the far wall, about a metre high, a good five metres from the windows. They walked to the end, to get as far from Jorge's combination of ablutionary and revolutionary fervour as they could.

Argand took a deep breath. Below he could now see a small swimming pool, flower beds filled with roses and tall scarlet and maroon lilies. Palm trees rose from the lawns, bougainvillaea and jasmine tumbled over walls and down trellises. The brown rock of San Cristóbal glowed orange in the last light above lilac mists, and a star or planet shone in the deepening blue of the clear sky above it.

He spoke as evenly as he could. "My case was stolen. The documents in it were passed on to the popular junta against the Base. Since it could be very difficult for me to prove that I did not deliberately allow this to happen, I will be discredited with my superiors as at least a security risk, and at the worst as some sort of leftie. I must protect myself. I must find out who is engineering this plot against me. Clearly you have played a most important part. . . ."

"Commissioner, I think you are mad." She said this quietly, but firmly, as if coming to a decision, and turned away from him. To follow her movement he turned too and found he was looking down the balcony and into her bathroom. The shutters were half open, the shower curtain adjusted to come between the bath and the door — Jorge was quite exposed to both of them and quite oblivious of them. The light was bright and unshaded. His body was twisted beneath the shower as he soaped his left buttock and the crack between. His genitalia, large and like ripe fruit swung with his movements beneath forests of black hair that stretched unbroken almost to his collar-bones.

130

"*Marchemos juntos al porvenir.*"

"And you are a whore," Argand shouted. "A filthy, evil whore."

Glowing white like a moon in the gloaming, a face on the balcony next door now lifted from the book it had been reading. Professor Shiner lifted a glass of sherry that caught the evening light. He said, in English, "Commissioner. We do seem destined to run into each other. Would you and Dr Brunot care to join me?"

"What is all this? What is the point of it all?" Argand stirred the papers on her table.

Surprised and mortified by the sudden storm of feeling that had overcome him, and by the fact that Shiner had seen it, if not understood, he had almost scurried back into the bedroom. Brunot hung behind for a second, exchanged a word or two with the Scot, then called to Jorge. The singing stopped. Now she sat on the bed, more embarrassed than horrified or frightened by the Commissioner's outburst, and wondered what on earth she could do with him. His question came as a relief. She came over, stood at his shoulder.

"Benítez wrote great books," she said. She spoke quickly but quietly, hoping to soothe him. "Like all great artists he was a questioner, a rebel. Dialectically exposing the false reality imposed on his society by the establishment of his time. And much, many of the evils he exposed are still with us. We haven't moved far out of the nineteenth century."

She indicated a large volume. *Las Dos Naciones.*

"Consequently he doesn't get the readings he needs. What I mean is, the academics, critics, and so on, who are institutionalized as part of the state, these people offer readings of Benítez that make it appear he was a supporter of the establishment of his own time, and where he was not, the abuses he revealed are now gone. They see that he is read as someone who upholds the values of civilization as we know it. In short they make

131

him say things he didn't say. Well, what I'm doing is looking at the accepted readings of this book, and I try to show how they twist the text away from what it was, create new texts from the same printed words, and I try to show how these new readings are conditioned, often quite unconsciously, not by the printed words, but by the deeply rooted beliefs of the people who are making them. I've tried to put it as simply as I can, but I don't suppose I've made much sense."

Argand too was anxious to keep things low-keyed for a time. His hands were shaking, he was still disgusted with himself — not because he had made a misjudgement, nor because he had been abominably rude, but because he had lost control.

"And what has this to do with it?" He pointed at, would not touch, *The Civil War in France*.

"*Las Dos Naciones* was written in 1884. But the action takes place between 1871 and 1874. Characters in it talk about the Paris Commune. One of them even claims to have read this. But the critics say that Benítez had only heard of it, not read it himself. You see they really need to believe he knew nothing more than hearsay of the works of this man. So I'm looking at it again to show that Benítez had read it. But it's not the only reason." Her tone became dryer, her enunciation crisper. "Believe it or not, the man who wrote this really did understand his times better than anyone else."

Argand again had to repress a shudder. He looked out of the window. The light was fading from San Cristóbal, the orange deepening to ambers, purple, black. Two or three stars now shone with the first planet in the indigo sky. The sound of the shower had stopped. Now they heard a nose blown furiously, with retching and spitting after — that part of southern ablutions that sounds so unpleasant to northern sensibilities. Argand felt he was still not quite sufficiently under control to return to the purpose of his visit.

132

"You really mean to tell me that people, trained and educated people, in the face of evidence as indisputable as what an author has actually set down in print, will make out he said quite different things?"

"Just that. None of us knows how what we believe is conditioned by forces beyond our control. Even the way we see, touch and hear owes more to what we believe than to the objective reality that stimulates our senses."

Argand found this too clever by half. "Nonsense. What we see we see; what we hear we hear."

"But it's a question of what we make of what we see and hear, isn't it? We see what we *need* to see. Life would be too constantly unsettling otherwise."

The bathroom door opened. Jorge appeared. His thick black hair was wet, there was a fresh pinkness about his face, a pinkness that shone through the thick black hair on his arms and chest. The whiteness of his shirt was startling in the diffused light that came from the reading lamp on the table. His smile was startling too.

"*Ya he terminado señora.*"

"*Muy bien. Ven cuando quieras.*"

"*Les pido perdón por lo del ruido. Es que tengo costumbre de cantar . . .*"

"*No tiene importancia, déjalo. La cosa es que estábamos hablando de algo, bueno, de algo importante. ¿Te veremos a la cena?*"

"*No señora. Tengo noche libre hoy. Voy a bajar a Las Guavas.*"

"*Pues, ¡ que te diviertas!*"

"*Gracias señora, Adiós.* Goodbye, Mister."

This last was said to Argand, with an even wider grin. Then he was gone.

There was a moment's silence.

Argand said: "He's taken your towel and shampoo."

"They are his. He brought them with him."

This silence was longer. From below they could have heard, had

133

they needed to, the irritatingly irregular tock-t-tock-t-tock of a ping-pong ball, followed by a small cheer. Then tock-t-tock-t-tock again. But Argand was aware only of Françoise's breathing which was suddenly audible and quickening.

"So that's why you called me a whore." Clearly she was now very angry indeed. "You thought Jorge had come here to make love with me, is that it?"

Argand said nothing.

"Commissioner, why do you *need* to think I am a whore? And the other things too. You should ask yourself, you really should. Jorge is a waiter here. The first night he served us I noticed that he smelt. Not badly, just not quite fresh. I asked him about it. There in no hot water where he lives and no means of heating it, and no private room where he can wash. So I told him that while I am here he can use this bathroom."

Argand was aware of a growing sense of wretchedness, of misery even. He looked away. Only the silhouette of San Cristóbal, a row of black and broken teeth, could now be seen against the sky, beneath the stars. But on the desk, the roses, pink and yellowish, glowed in the light from the lamp. Then quite suddenly a petal dropped, lay like a feather on Françoise Brunot's book, *The Civil War in France*. Argand determined in that instant to pay Joachim a visit.

"I'll go now." He picked up his hat, and the newspaper *El Obrero Virtuoso*.

"Yes. I'd like it if you would. Commissioner, it was no accident I passed on your papers. It was a duty. But it *was* an accident that your case came into my hands. That little Indian man who came up here expecting me to have his was quite certain of that. Will you accept that for the truth it is and stop pestering me? Right?"

She held the door for him and he went.

XV

TAXIS were no longer available. Argand had been lucky to get a lift in the Congress bus, for the *Residencia Universitaria* was eight kilometres up in the hills behind Las Guavas. Now there was nothing for it but the regular bus service. Yes, that was running. The point of the strike was to inconvenience the bosses, not the ordinary people. The bus stop was on the main road, just down the hill.

So much Argand learned from the *jefe* of the residence, a huge man with spectacles, a sad face, and an obvious desire to help everyone. Moreover he spoke French.

Argand joined a short queue on the roadside above a very steep drop, really a small cliff, set on a hairpin bend. A naked bulb fastened to a metal girder telephone post cast a garish light over them and giant white moths blundered into it. Large cars went by, tyres squealing, horns blaring, filling the warm air with fumes. In the gaps between, the heavy fragrance of jasmine and something sharper, cat-like, came through strongly. Somewhere up the road there was a café. Its lights glowed in the acacia foliage above it. A guitar tinkled and hands clapped.

The bus came, blaring its horn at the corner, air-brakes and doors exploding and hissing. Pay at the door. Argand fumbled for change but the driver waved his finger in front of his face, and over the pile of small coins that lay scattered on a baize cloth across the engine-housing. A voice murmured in his ear, in French.

"Your fare is paid, sir. By the gentleman in the third seat."

Argand looked down the bus. Jorge's wide white grin flashed at him, followed by a fine wave of the hand — a hidalgo disclaiming the necessity for thanks. Fortunately a pretty girl was sitting beside him, there was no obligation to sit with him. Argand passed down the bus and the neat little man who had spoken to him came and sat across the gangway from him. With doors hissing shut, and horn blaring again the bus pulled out into the path of an Alfa Romeo.

"Why did he do that?" asked Argand. "Why did he pay my fare?"

"He told the driver you are a foreigner, that you would not know the fare, so he would pay."

"How did he know where I was going?"

"It's a single charge. Twenty pesetas no matter how far you go."

"I still don't really understand why he paid for me."

"The islanders are like that. Simple people. Very kind, and always ready to be friendly. The poorer ones, anyway."

The bus rushed on through the warm dark. Lights flashed by — houses, villas, cars coming and going. Everywhere there seemed to be blossom, though the way the artificial lights shone on the leaves may have made some of them look like flowers. The bus was almost full. Most of the passengers were young — the men almost all dressed in immaculately white shirts, the girls in colourful dresses with scarves on their heads. There was a strong smell of cheap but naturally scented colognes. There was a lot of laughter, much animated gossip, and four of them, two couples in the back seat, were crooning a song. Others joined in.

Poblador compañero poblador
Seguiremos avanzando hasta el final . . .

"I am not an islander myself, though I have lived here for twenty years. I am from Pamplona." This was said with pride. Argand looked across the gangway again. The small man was tubby, had dark hair well smoothed back, a wide round face, and blue eyes which twinkled.

"I am a school teacher. Since 1936 we Basques have not been allowed to teach our own people, so we teach the rest of Spain instead. Of course things have changed, but it's too late for me to go back now. I suppose you are here on holiday — have you rented one of the villas?"

"No. No, I am working here for a time." Basque, Cro-Magnon Man. For a second Argand could see nothing but skulls, like footballs. Then, with a note of pride in his voice, he added: "I am connected with the Base."

The Basque's brows contracted. He looked out of the window. But his sociableness and curiosity got the better of him and he soon turned back. "What did you think of the march and demonstration, then? It was a big affair, eh? I have never seen so many on the streets of Las Guavas. Twice, three times the crowds when *Los Reyes* came, Juan Carlos and Sofia."

"The demonstration was not against the Base. It was against the use of the French digger."

"Yes, that's true, that's very true. There would not have been so many if it had been simply against the Base."

At each stop more people got on than got off. Now there was standing room only and a short but very broad sallow-skinned lady in a tight dress swayed between them and carried on a loud conversation with her gossip at the other end of the bus. This didn't deter the Basque. He leant round her backside and carried on.

"I thought the authorities handled it well. They're cunning bastards. I mean that bit about stopping work until it was all settled. They know there's not enough work as it is."

Argand allowed himself a private smile, a touch smug.

"Of course I'm against the Base myself. No offence, we're all entitled to our opinions. Well, we are now, for a time. We weren't for forty years, and maybe in the future we won't be again, but just now we can think what we like, eh?"

"Why are you against the Base?" Argand was drawn in spite of himself. "The whole point of it is that it will help protect this freedom you are talking of."

"Oh? Is that what it's for? Well, it might work like that for other people elsewhere but it won't do that here."

"I don't understand."

"It's very simple." The Basque twisted in his seat so he could nearly face Argand. He began to use his fingers to mark off the points he was making. "That Base is going to have rockets with nuclear warheads. It's going to have the most secret electronic devices ever invented. Hidden in there will be all the Yankee plans for aggression and counter-aggression. With that lot under our noses, or above our heads on the top of San Cristóbal, we're going to be watched and monitored and kept track of like no population ever has been before. Every word or gesture that anyone makes against the Base will be put on record. There will be spies and secret police everywhere, files on everyone."

"I don't think it will be as bad as that."

"Oh yes it will. It stands to reason. Do you think that once the Yankees have built that place they are going to allow opposition to it? Or permit people to live normal lives who might think it their duty to pass on information to the Russkies or whoever? No. If you're against the Base you might as well get out for all the chance you'll have of a decent normal *free* life on Santa Caridad. Well, that's the way I see it anyway."

He looked out of the window for a bit, then turned back. "And I can't go back to my village in Navarre either. They're building a fast-breeder nuclear reactor on the river just above it. It'll ruin the fishing, and we'll be watched like criminals there too."

The bus roared on down countless hairpin bends, and the lights of Las Guavas swung up to them. Soon the road broadened into a

138

wide urban highway, well lit and slicing through the shanty towns on the outskirts. The Basque turned back.

"Where are you staying then?"

"Hotel Santa Teresa."

"My goodness you must be quite a high-up then. I'm sorry — took you for a foreman, something of that sort."

Argand was annoyed at this. In spite of the man's opinions he liked the Basque, saw him as a decent, straightforward sort of person.

"I'm not really a high-up," he said. "I just happen to be an expert in one side of the business, that's all." He stopped, hoping that the Basque, would *not* ask what aspect of it all he was connected with. After what he had said it would have been embarrassing to have to admit he was in fact an adviser on security.

But the Basque had something of his own on his mind. He ruminated for a minute or so, then said: "Well, you must be in touch with the bosses, staying there, have access to them I mean."

"Yes. I suppose I have."

"Well, you tell them from me that they're all wrong about these bank raids. They're nothing to do with the Junta Popular, nothing at all. Don't get me wrong. I don't know about the raids, but I do know about the Junta. I'm the delegate and convener for our village, and I can tell you this — to say we have anything to do with robbing banks is just crazy."

Argand was silent and the bus roared on. Then the Basque pulled and tugged at something he had in his jacket pocket.

"And you can give this back to the owners too." He passed the object across the narrow gangway, and the fat lady in black looked down at it as he did so. It was a brick-red cylinder about eight inches long and an inch and a half in diameter. It was heavy, half a kilo at least, and, in spite of the rubberized surface, hard. "They were firing these into the crowd at the end, you know. I was lucky.

This just got me a glancing one on the thigh, but I'll have the bruise for weeks. Lucky it didn't break my leg or have my balls off."

"*Son hijos de putas, todos,*" said the woman. "*Porras, escudos y esa puerca máquina — lo tienen todo menos cojones, ¿verdad?*"

"*Tiene razón señora, eso que sí.*"

"I don't want it," Argand said.

"No, you take it. You just give it back to them nicely, and tell them they can find some other use for such obscenities, they'll know what I mean, instead of firing them at poor people whose only fault is that they don't want to be the first casualties in the next war."

They were in a wide, brightly lit avenue now, clearly near the centre of Las Guavas. Although Argand had not been there at night he recognized a large roundabout, with a fountain in the middle. Then the bus pulled in to the curb.

"This is as far as we go," said the Basque. "The bus turns round here and goes back. But it's not far to the Santa Teresa. Ten minutes walk at the most."

Chattering brightly the passengers piled out on to the pavement. They had come down from their villages for a night out — the cinema, the bars near the ocean, perhaps just to walk slowly down the boulevards, looking at the shops and the clubs, following that most Spanish of institutions, the *paseo*. Argand checked a sign on a street corner. He was right — Avenida de Venezuela.

"Goodbye, Mister," said a voice at his elbow — and again Jorge grinned and waved, and then sauntered off, hand in hand with his girl, into the crowd. Argand felt a tug at his sleeve. The boy who had followed him to the *Museo* grinned up at him.

"*Pase señor,*" he said, "*pase pase.*" And he led him to the block numbered thirty-three. Argand was already on his way there.

XVI

IT was a large building, faced in pale ochre stone, with a large entrance, a double door framed in stainless steel, set between an art dealer and a specialist in oriental rugs. The foyer was done out in rose-coloured marble and a janitor looked out from an illuminated Perspex box. Argand found a card, on it he wrote "Joachim Joachim, 4E", the janitor nodded, took the card, pressed a buzzer and waited. A voice answered, a woman's. There was another wait, the voice murmured again.

"*Muy bien, puede subir, señor,*" said the janitor. Argand hesitated, the janitor said again, more loudly: "*Muy bien, puede subir.*" He raised his hand slowly, like a lift.

A maid opened Joachim's door. "*Pase, pase,*" she said.

Argand followed her down a short corridor. It was thickly carpeted, lit by dim lamps that glowed behind small clusters of crystal drops. The scent of a heavy cologne hung over everything, not quite covering the smells of stale, spicy cooking. She showed him into a small sitting-room furnished with a three-piece suite in heavy bottle green velvet. There were velvet curtains to match, a small table and a sideboard, both black inlaid with mother-of-pearl. Carved alabaster reproductions of Michelangelo's David and the Medici Venus stood on the sideboard. This room too was lit, and again not brightly, by a crystal chandelier. Argand was about to lift the edge of the curtain, to see what the outlook of the room was, when he heard the sigh of the door over the deep carpet and the click of the latch as it closed.

141

"Commissioner. Won't you sit down?"

Joachim looked paler, perhaps not quite so huge, though this may have been because he was now wearing a dark, almost black suit and a black tie. He stood looking at Argand for a moment or two. Then he said: "Did Pedro find you? Or have you come of your own accord?"

"Pedro? The boy downstairs? Yes, he found me."

"He's a good boy."

"But I was coming anyway."

Joachim nodded, then lowered himself into the large chair. He motioned Argand towards the sofa.

Argand cleared his throat: "I'll come straight to the point. I think now that it is possible that your stepson exchanged cases with me accidentally. That it was all a mistake."

For some time Joachim did not speak or move. The silence was quite unbroken — only by straining his ears could Argand pick up the seemingly very distant sounds of the traffic from the avenue.

When the gem dealer did speak it was very quietly, so that Argand involuntarily leant forward to catch what he said.

"Two questions arise, sir. First — why have you changed your mind on a matter about which you were adamant? Second — why have you come here to tell me so?"

Argand thought: I cannot say that I changed my mind because a man I thought was a gigolo turned out to be a waiter who wanted to be clean on his night off.

"I will try to answer the second question first. You said, at our last meeting, that your main concern now is to bring the murderers of your stepson to book. If this is the truth then I think I am under an obligation to help you. First because I know that the police of Las Guavas are not going to make any great effort to find the murderers, and I happen to think that murderers should be caught, no matter who they are. Secondly, if your stepson's case

142

came into my possession entirely as the result of an accident then I acted foolishly. And it may be that that foolishness was a contributory cause of his death.

"As to why I have changed my mind, well, that's a little more difficult to explain. I hope you will be satisfied if I say that since we met I have gone over it all in my mind, and I now see that what I thought had happened need not have been the case at all."

Joachim made a church of his podgy fingers and slowly rubbed the tips over his chins. His eyes looked more hooded than ever. He spoke slowly: "Sir, you must forgive me if I question you closely. Salim was working for me. You say his case had heroin in it. The penalties for trafficking in heroin are very severe. I must assure myself that you are not part of a plot to ruin me, to send me to prison for what would, I am sure, be, the rest of my life. We must go over all the ground. In detail."

"This is not going to be pleasant. I acted foolishly, and I do not easily admit to being a fool."

Joachim's hands separated in a gesture that looked not unlike that used by priests offering absolution. Argand went on.

"At Barajas there was a bomb-scare. In the confusion I lost my case. Others may also have done so. I picked up one that was identical and I took it back to the plane. Between Madrid and Santa Caridad I had no reason to open it until just before we landed. At that point I realized that it was not mine. It occurred to me it could be another bomb. On landing the plane was evacuated. A bomb disposal team opened the case and found in it three kilos of heroin."

"Was there anything else?"

"Yes. A magazine. I should have said your stepson sat next to me as far as Madrid. He offered me the magazine, or one very like it, and I refused."

Perhaps a note of distaste had crept into his voice.

143

"I can imagine the sort of thing it was. In some ways he was immature. Poor boy. And the case then remained in police custody?"

"Yes."

"Go on."

Argand took a deep breath. "Well. In Brabt I have enemies. They are powerful people and I am a threat to them. When I was told that the case that had been planted on me contained heroin I thought that they had concocted a plot to frame me. This may sound far-fetched, but I repeat, the cases were identical, the same make, the same in every way. I still find that a coincidence hard to swallow."

"What did you do then?"

"I thought: I must take what steps I can to pin this conspiracy on the people who were responsible. It seemed to me that one way I could do this would be to question Salim. But before I could trace his address I discovered that he was following me. It was not difficult therefore to . . . interview him on his own. I tried . . . I tried to persuade him to tell me who had instructed him to plant the heroin on me. But he broke free before . . ."

"You beat him, I think. There were still bruises around his mouth that were older than the far more serious injuries that led to his death. His arrest followed, and through that you found out his full name and his connection with me?"

"That's more or less right. In fact he gave me your name. Later Pérez, the police chief here, told me that you are a gem dealer suspected of smuggling."

"Did he?" Joachim pursed his lips. "Did he indeed? And how did you find out the addresses, in Cervantes and here?"

"I have access to CRIC."

"I know about CRIC. You cabled and you got an express reply. I see. What else?"

144

"Four nights ago, just after I received the CRIC reports, an intruder broke into my room at the Santa Teresa. He was an experienced thug. Naturally I thought he was connected with you."

"He was not, sir. What happened?"

"There was a struggle. He escaped through the window. But in the struggle he left this."

Argand opened his fist. On the palm was the glass eye he had trodden and almost tumbled on. Joachim turned it with his finger.

"That at least is something. I think I can see now some of what happened. But I am not yet entirely convinced of your neutrality towards me. Salim should not have been carrying heroin. I did not expect him to be and he did not expect it either. I too have enemies — I must convince myself that all this, including your presence here now, is not part of some ingenious way of framing *me*."

Having recognized how his own fears had stood between him and the truth, it was now particularly frustrating to find that they were likely to be balked by similar fears on Joachim's part. Argand strove to master this irritation, to keep his voice clam. "Well. I put myself in your hands. But I, we, have been involved in a complex of events that neither of us understands, and they led to your step-son's death. We both have good reasons, personal and involving our duty to society, to try to unravel them."

Joachim was silent, then he breathed in deeply. The air rumbled in the passages and caverns of his chest.

"You are in Las Guavas as Internal Security adviser to IBOBRAS regarding this Base that they are building for the Americans."

"That is correct."

"And for no other reason."

"No."

"And everything you did in connection with this heroin, and

with Salim, was done because you believed you were to be framed as a smuggler of heroin."

"Yes."

"It is difficult to believe."

"But . . ."

"No need to go over it all again. The cases. Identical. Your enemies. And so on. Tell me: why was Salim arrested?"

"After the case was found to contain heroin I was questioned as to how it might have come into my possession. I have told you . . ."

"Yes. He sat next to you. And then there was the magazine. No doubt the police identified him from your description. But why did they not arrest him straightaway?"

"I suppose because they could not find him. Yes. That is what I was told."

"That is nonsense, sir. The police in Las Guavas knew Salim very well. They knew where to find him."

Again he made a church out of his fingers. His eyelids flickered behind them. The silence grew deeper; Argand began to wonder if the huge man had gone to sleep or withdrawn into a self-induced trance. At last the great head lifted and the sigh came again.

"Well sir. I am disposed to believe you. You have a reputation. And after all I have little left to hope for, little to lose. My wife, you understand, Salim's mother . . . That is by the way. They arrested Salim very shortly after you had seen him. I think that is significant. It must be. Well sir. You have been frank with me. More than last time we met. It is time for me to reciprocate, then perhaps together we may be able to do something about bringing retribution on poor Salim's torturers and murderers." He heaved himself to his feet. "However, I am feeling peckish and I think you may be too. I am sure María will have eggs, cold meat and so on. Would you like me to see if she can manage a *petit souper* for us? I should also like to think things over for half an hour — I can do that while we eat."

Argand was aware that he was indeed very hungry. He had had nothing since midday and then he had eaten little — all that had been offered in the Saviem command vehicle was cold potato omelette served as a sandwich in Spanish loaves. Joachim rang the bell again and issued orders to the maid; then he took Argand to a dining-room furnished with a dark, heavy, reproduction table and chairs. From a huge sideboard the gem dealer took a pair of elaborately cut crystal glasses and poured sherry from an equally ornate decanter. In a solid silver frame was a photo — a handsome dark-haired woman in a sari with her arm round a youth. Salim.

"There should be some . . . pistachios. Do you like them? I am afraid my wife will not join us. You understand of course. She is very upset by recent events."

Argand sipped the sherry and nibbled the nuts. It became suddenly quite difficult to resist the temptation to scoop up a handful and eat them out of the palm of his hand. He looked around, took in his surroundings in more detail. On a low table near him there was a brochure for a residential development of apartments and villas near the Cap d'Agde in the south of France.

"I have an interest in that," said Joachim, following his glance. "In fact we, my wife and I, shall be retiring to a villa we have nearby just as soon as this business is over. It was foolish of me not to go before, and that foolishness has cost my poor stepson his life. I must see that that debt is paid."

The maid reappeared and briskly served them with cold meats, eggs in mayonnaise, black olives and white floury bread. They shared a half bottle of very cold white wine, then she brought coffee in.

"We can stay here I think? Right. I shall begin at the beginning. Though first let me say that I think you are mistaken about one

147

thing. Salim changed the cases on purpose. But we'll come to that in its proper place."

"Commissioner, I am a gem dealer, and occasionally I have carried out transactions and arranged the movement of gems in contravention of the laws of more than one country. Indeed I could be charged in eight or nine different places. Though not in Santa Caridad. Here the police are corrupt and I have bought them. If they moved against me here I would bring them down with me. I think this fact may be material to what we are involved in now, but that is by the way.

"I feel no guilt about this. The laws regarding the marketing of gems are designed solely to protect the interests of people who are already very wealthy — and yet what I have done has, as often as not, been done for these very same people, usually to assist them in tax evasion or similar frauds. So. My activities have harmed no one in any appreciable way.

"Six months ago I was on the point of retiring — most of my assets had already been transferred to the real estate and development that brochure represents. Salim was to return to Gibraltar where he was born, and where I had bought him a small business, a chain of dry cleaners in fact. Then things began to go wrong.

"First, one of my couriers, a steward on a cruise boat, was arrested in Southampton. I had to reimburse a client, and pay a pension to the steward's wife for four years. Then another customer received a diamond that turned out not to be genuine, and he too had to be reimbursed. This was serious, for in this trade mutual trust is essential, and the reliability of my wares had been impugned. There were other incidents. I shall not bore you with the details, but putting them all together, and discarding the possibility of coincidence, they indicated that my organization had been uncovered by a law enforcement agency with considerable resources. No single individual could have attacked me at such widely differing points. I suspected the South Africans — there were indications that suggested that a common factor in each of these disasters was the South African end of my operations.

"A question. If a law enforcement agency had penetrated my organization, why was it now robbing me instead of bringing me to book? The answer soon became apparent.

"Telephone calls were followed by clandestine meetings with people I had never met before and have not seen since. It was made clear to me that my entire operation had been uncovered, that four or five loyal and long-serving employees were in danger of summary arrest. There was even some danger to me personally. But I could ward off Nemesis if I did as I was told. In short, sir, I was to be blackmailed.

"I was asked to guarantee a draft of a quarter of a million pounds on the Banco de Santa Caridad for a period of two weeks. The money was to finance a coup or revolution and I would be repaid when it had succeeded. Now those who put out their money for this sort of venture never do so at less than two hundred per cent, and they expect to lose it two times out of three. I was offered no interest at all. Just the return of my principal if, *if* all went well.

"I assumed, rightly I think, that the country involved shares borders with South Africa, that the South Africans are using a method of financing a change in government in one of their neighbours that owes something to their American cousins. That is, they are using law enforcement agencies to uncover operations like mine and then blackmailing them to put up funds they dare not be seen to be providing themselves. No doubt my quarter of a million is only part of a wider net.

"That amount was well chosen for it very nearly matches the sort of sum I should have been able to realize quite quickly a year ago. But by the time they were in touch with me I had already

149

realized the assets in question and invested them in this project on the Cap d'Agde. This had been done discreetly. The laundering of such sums is no longer easy, but I have resources. The upshot was that I simply no longer had the quarter million these people had set their minds on, and to realize it again, even to borrow money against it, would have taken months, so well had I covered my tracks.

"An impasse then. The threat to my organization did not bother me — as you have gathered I was already winding it up. But the threat to my employees did. After so many years I could not think of them going to prison and yet it seemed at times inevitable that they would. The people I was dealing with made it clear that arrests were imminent.

"However, their plans were too well advanced and could not be reversed. Such is the case with revolutions, relying as they do, to some extent, on mobilizing quite large bodies of people whose motivation is emotional and ephemeral — it seemed after that a lot depended on this draft on the Banco de Santa Caridad being guaranteed. They could not find anyone at short notice to take my place and the upshot was that they said my people would be reprieved on two conditions. First, I should wind up and cease operating. I was happy to agree. Second, I should send my most trusted courier to Amsterdam where he would take delivery of gems equivalent in value to a quarter of a million. I should take these to the bank, accompanied by an independent valuer, and deposit them there as security against the draft. Since I believed that the South Africans were ultimately at the bottom of it all, this seemed very satisfactory. The gems would be diamonds, and not stolen. There was no longer any financial risk for me. I was happy to agree.

"Salim took delivery following a procedure we had employed before. What follows is conjecture. On the plane I believe he learnt that there was to be a baggage search at Madrid. And then you say the case held not gems but heroin. He was very frightened I'm sure, but kept his head sufficiently to follow a plan to be used only as a last resort to avoid certain arrest — one we had never yet had to employ — namely swapping cases with anyone around who carried a similar article of luggage, and then, if that person got through, swapping back again. It was a rough and ready plan and we did not really expect it to work completely; that is, if we ever had to use it we expected to lose the goods, but at least avoid the courier's arrest.

"Possibly Salim sat next to you because your cases were alike. I imagine he elicited from you that your destination was Las Guavas. Then, on the second leg, he failed to make the swap back. . . ." (Argand explained how he had transferred to the first class.) ". . . here in Santa Caridad he watched you, and no doubt watched the newspapers and so on as well. There was no report of heroin being found on the plane, and so he must have presumed that you had decided to keep it. Then you caught him, and . . . questioned him. He was arrested the same evening and questioned, more officially, by the police."

He paused. In the silence Argand could hear the traffic again, and distantly the sound of the maid working in the kitchen — washing up the few plates and so on that they had used. Joachim leaned across the table and went on.

"He was apparently released through lack of evidence, but he was not seen again alive. He was not seen until I found him dead in his Calle Cervantes attic. Now, sir. In the other room I said I was disposed to believe you. For that reason I instructed Pedro, who was keeping an eye on you for me, to bring you here. I also said that I saw a connection between your meeting with Salim and his arrest."

Argand felt a touch of anticipatory dread. Suddenly he could see where the argument was leading. Joachim's voice took on an edge it had lacked before.

"They arrested him because they were afraid he could tell you, *perhaps had told you*, something they did not want you to know."

Argand licked his lips. "The police. Pérez."

"Perhaps Pérez. You will know better than I. And they tortured him to get him to reveal what he had told you."

"But he told me nothing. Nothing material."

"What could he have told you if you had asked?"

Argand's mind jumped. Things were coming clearer with every second. It was as if he had been looking at a puzzle, a picture that made no sense, but it was not a question of fitting in parts — they were already there and fitted. It was as if the trick was to reverse the picture, look at it from the back or upside down — then it made sense.

"He told me that he was given the case at Amsterdam airport. That normally he simply picked it up. I could have asked him to describe the man."

"And his murderers knew that if he had you would have identified the man from the description. I have known for some time that someone senior in the Las Guavas police was involved." Joachim was speaking more quickly now, as if hurrying on to an end both of them could guess at. "The day after your arrival I was approached. Just a phone-call. I was asked if I would accept heroin as a guarantee of my loan instead of gems. I refused. I will not handle the stuff. It was impractical anyway: the bank which knows I no longer have liquid assets in Las Guavas would have accepted gems from me as a guarantee — it would hardly have taken heroin. Then in Salim's attic you told me that the case, which the police had, contained heroin. I do not believe in coincidences. Now, from that point I could begin to see that you were not directly involved with whatever was going on. It became clearer that you were acting counter

152

to it, albeit unwittingly. And that is why I became disposed to believe you. Because of that and your reputation."

"You had made enquiries about me before we met."

"Yes. You see we had a rule that if anything goes wrong with a courier he breaks contact with me. I of course know that he has done so and I then begin to look into what has happened from my side, but without directly implicating myself. I have resources. I discovered you sat next to Salim on the plane. I heard about the bomb at Barajas. It seemed likely that he had swapped cases with you and failed to swap back. And so you became a puzzle — the Honest Commissioner who had come into possession of a quarter of a million pounds worth of gems and was keeping them to himself."

"But it was heroin, not gems. Why?"

"That is something we have yet to discover. Perhaps the gems failed to come through. If, as I suppose, more than one law enforcement agency is involved they would have had as ready access to heroin."

"A quarter of a million. It would be for arms . . ."

"And bribes too."

"There was an arms dealer here in Las Guavas."

"Trencher? Yes. I think he was the man. Transfer of ownership of arms is often made in Las Guavas. He has been here before. With the facilities of the free port such transactions are more easily and legally effected here than . . ."

"And you are sure the police, Pérez perhaps, are involved?"

"There is no other explanation of all the facts. I know you were followed by police, I know . . ."

"Then I think I understand almost everything." Argand felt no sense of exhilaration as he said this, rather exhaustion and despair at the thought of what lay ahead. "You see, with me too it is a rule of thumb never to allow the possibility of coincidence. But several

153

days ago I did — because if I had ruled out coincidence I would have been left, as I am now, with the unthinkable."

"Go on."

"Trencher too was offered the heroin as payment for his arms. He refused. I actually saw it happen."

A girl with red hair, stockings, and nothing else. His mind had been unable to accept that the magazine Enrique Cortés had angrily thrown on one side had in fact been Salim's — not just another copy of the same magazine, or one like it, but Salim's, and the case that had been on the table between the banker and Trencher had been Salim's too.

XVII

LATER the Governor, the commander of the garrison, the chief of the Civil Guard, and numerous officials both from the islands and the mainland were unanimous that a unilateral declaration of independence would have had no chance of success, not even one supported by a considerable body of well-armed men. The people, they said, the ordinary islanders would have had no truck with it at all. They were loyal to Juan Carlos and mainland Spain. Consider, they said, how recently they had demonstrated that loyalty during the latest official visit of *Los Reyes*. But it was conceded that there would have been far more bloodshed than there was had not the plot been discovered in the nick of time, that is a matter of hours before the rebel forces were to be deployed and the *pronunciamiento* made over *Radio Popular de las Guavas*.

Throughout the early hours and morning of the seventh of September things seemed to be going well for the rebels. The difficulties they had encountered in financing the arms deal with Trencher had been solved by the expedient of removing the necessary sums from the Banco de Santa Caridad in a series of simultaneous bank raids. Señor Enrique Cortés, a deputy director of the bank who expected to be finance minister in the new government, arranged these, and, knowing that the notes and specie had already been returned to the vaults, was then able, with one or two scarcely detectable adjustments in the books, to offer the bank's own guarantee on the draft that had been drawn for Trencher. It was now immediately negotiable in London, and as soon as it had been cleared — just before the close of business on the sixth — Trencher's shipping agent signed the documents that secured the release of the container from the bonded part of the port.

The dock gates opened at six in the morning and Pérez, who expected the portfolio for home affairs, was there to authorize the normally illegal transfer of arms from the port to the interior of the island. He was accompanied by Señor Cortés, who now held the title to the contents of the container.

As they stood there in the pearly dawn, a white Rolls-Royce — its right wing scarred — drew up alongside Cortés' Mercedes. Carlos, Guzmán's bastard son, was driving. He also expected a senior post in the new government, though just what had not been decided — a wag had suggested Grand Inquisitor. In the back sat Commissioner Argand, who had been lost since he disappeared into the Museo de Santa Caridad ahead of his followers. Pérez was relieved to see him, but puzzled when Carlos described how he had appeared at the Santa Teresa only twenty minutes earlier, had seen Carlos in the Rolls, and had calmly opened the back door and got in. Since then he had said nothing. It was the first sign, barely more than a hint, that not everything was quite as it should be.

The dock gates opened, the container, now on the back of a San Salvador SA truck, was passed out, and the little convoy made its way through the suburbs and up into the hills. The sun was well up by the time they reached the finca and there was a lot to be done. The foreign commissioner was bundled away into an upstairs bedroom and to all intents and purposes forgotten; though Pérez detailed an officer back in town to find out where he had been since they had lost him outside the museum. It did occur to him that the commissioner might have made contact with Joachim Joachim.

So, all in all, Pérez was not happy about it. He would have liked to have spent a lot more time than he had available questioning Commissioner Argand. Clearly the European IS expert had stumbled on a considerable part of the plot — no doubt he had been ferreting away at it ever since the wretched business with his case had occurred at Barajas — but he never found out how much Argand knew, who else he had told, nor, above all, just why the Commissioner had allowed himself to be so easily taken.

Pérez actually thought for a time that Argand might be hoping for some sort of post in the new government in exchange for his silence.

Still, in the general scheme of things, Argand's odd behaviour seemed to be a matter of little importance. Most aspects of the plot were going as they had hoped. Five hundred men of the Legion were landed in the port where they remained with ten Cadillac Gage V-150 armoured cars mounted with 90mm Cockerill cannon. The Governor was apparently angry about these, he had expected the legionaries to arrive from Santa Prudencia with troop carriers only. He could not see why they needed mobile light artillery to escort the digger from the port to the Base, nor why they should have arrived a full twenty-four hours before they were required, but he agreed it would be silly to order them back and allowed them to stay, provided they remained within the port gates.

It was the eve of the Nativity of Our Lady and a large section of the population was already moving up to her shrine in the hills between Guzmán's finca and San Cristóbal, just as they always did. They came in cars, in coaches, many on foot not because of poverty but as penitents or votaries; some were even in helicopters which dropped rose petals on the crowds beneath, in honour of Our Lady and by courtesy of the largest department store in Las Guavas. To cope with it all Pérez moved three of his five hundred

157

regular riot police into the neighbourhood of the shrine using his buses and the GKN Sankey AT-104s — so much was routine, the same every year. What was new was the deployment of the rest of his regulars in a village not far from the finca. When the commander of the Civil Guard, in whose jurisdiction they now were, queried this move, Pérez answered that he hoped not to have to use them, but had moved them into the area in case. What he did not tell his colleague was that they had with them ten Panhard M3 VTT armoured personnel carriers and that during the course of the morning these were driven in pairs to the finca where armourers from the Legion fitted them with 20mm cannon and 60mm Hotchkiss Brandt mortars taken from Trencher's container. This also turned the Panhards into mobile light artillery — as such they were driven across country to a eucalyptus and mimosa grove which lay across the main road between the barracks and Las Guavas. It was expected that they would be enough to keep the inexperienced conscripts out of the picture while the legionaries occupied key places in the town.

By eleven-thirty things had gone so well that a number of the conspirators were arguing that the timing of the *pronunciamiento* should be advanced from six o'clock in the evening to four or even three o'clock. Only one thing so far had not happened as they had planned (apart from the mysterious appearance of the Brabanter policeman) — Colonel Javier de la Cerda had not left Santa Prudencia. Until he arrived on Santa Caridad the legionaries in the port were commanded by a major who was sympathetic to the plot but would not move on his own. The presence of de la Cerda was thought to be vital for other reasons too — he was a romantic figure, popular with the petty bourgeois of the town, the poujadists and small-time shopkeepers who admired his flamboyance, his scars, his missing right hand, and his defiance of metropolitan authority. The legionaries had been ready to die for him in the Sahara — would probably do so again, especially if a limited amount of looting in the duty-free luxury shops down the Calle Mayor was thrown in as a bonus.

He was to arrive at Benítez airport by helicopter at eleven o'clock, ostensibly on his way to Madrid, but there, instead of taking the scheduled LADI flight, he would transfer to one of Pérez's three Sikorsky helicopters and join his men at the port. And now, at eleven-thirty, he was still, as far as anyone at the finca knew, on Santa Prudencia. At the same time another minor hitch occurred — about thirty *congresistas*, those staying at the university residence, arrived at the finca in a coach. Someone had forgotten to cancel the reception they had been invited to.

Four times between eleven and eleven-thirty Pérez spoke to the Sikorsky pilot at Benítez, and each time the pilot reported that no army helicopter had arrived from Santa Prudencia. Then, at eleven-thirty-five the radio link with the airport fell silent. Pérez's radio operator tuned into the air control wave-lengths and learned that Benítez had been closed. Planes going out had apparently been grounded, incoming flights were being re-routed to the second of Las Virtudes — Santa Fe, which lay a hundred miles away below the horizon.

Then the officer who had been tracing Argand's movements the night before made his report and Pérez decided that he should have spent more time with the Commissioner than he had.

The spare bedroom Argand had been put in was small but pleasant — lit by the sun, with white walls, a wooden bed with carved ends, and above it a reproduction of an Infanta by Velázquez. He was pleased to see her; the serenity of her smile, the royalty of her pose seemed to him to stand for the essential rightness of things — the social order and so on — and he took her presence as a sign that things would work out all right.

159

There was a window and he spent most of the four hours he was there looking out of it. The view was a good one. Across rolling hills he could see the crest of San Cristóbal, and the gleaming white and silver of the complex of telescopes and communications systems, and he noted the changing colours of the ochre and red rock and scree as the sun climbed and the mists lifted. Palm and eucalyptus groves filled much of the middle ground. Over them buzzed a helicopter and rockets occasionally exploded, but fireworks only. He judged that these marked the position of the shrine and the build-up of the crowds that would gather through the day — until news of the attempted coup at last broke. That it would be an attempt only, an unsuccessful attempt, he had no doubt.

Meanwhile in the foreground, or, rather, immediately below him, glimpsed through the thin black cypresses that clung to the almost vertical terraces, lay the yard where Peters had parked on the day of the barbecue. In the middle was the container — odd how these look small when parked and stacked at a dock-side or in a marshalling yard, how enormous this one now seemed amongst ancient farm buildings that had never seen anything much larger than a two-ton truck carrying fodder or collecting manure.

A group of men, some in army overalls, some in blue monos were unloading it, breaking open cases, unwrapping the contents from stout oiled paper and cotton waste packing, and wiping down the rocket launchers, the mortars, and assembling the ten larger guns that were to be mounted on the Panhards. Twice during the morning they were visited by Carlos. On the second occasion he had changed into combat fatigues, a black beret and a black eye patch, and Argand smiled grimly to see him thus. More than ever was he now sure that this was the man who had broken into his room, the man who had stumbled over the trolley on his blind side during the bank raid, the servant who had been equally clumsy with a platter of steak and spoiled Professor Shiner's suit at the

160

barbecue. No doubt Guzmán's Rolls was scarred for the same reason.

The way it all fell into place was bringing with it a sense of euphoria — now he had time to think it all over, fit in new strands, place other hints whose relevance he had not at first noticed. For instance it was important — was it not? — that Salvador Guzmán had not been awarded the main contract for the Base, that it had gone to the metropolitan IBOBRAS, itself a subsidiary of multinational EUROSTRUCT. San Salvador SA was in trouble. There had been a large indemnity to pay on the airport runway, the hotel boom with its concomitant services — roads, drainage, water supply and so on — had collapsed. Guzmán, Joachim had asserted, was on the point of a particularly painful bankruptcy, painful because he was a vain pretentious man who traced his ancestry back through the Spanish side of his Argentinian forbears to the *conquistadores*, on the English side claimed a connection with the Wellesleys, and whose wife was an Alba. There were creditors in Las Guavas who would not forget his highhandedness when the crash came.

And Pérez, Guzmán's son-in-law. No wonder Pérez had been curious about Argand's connection with Salim for they could hardly have thought that Argand came by the heroin entirely unwittingly and by accident. And if, early on, he had convinced Pérez that this was the case, they must have been alerted to danger again when Argand continually asked about Salim, made contact with him, and finally discovered him dead. No wonder Pérez had kept Argand under close surveillance.

One question remained — if Joachim was right — who was it had given Salim the heroin at Amsterdam? Was it really someone Argand might have identified? For whose sake had Salim been tortured and murdered? Argand grew grim again as he thought of this. How much had Pérez had to do with Salim's death? Perhaps

161

after all not much, not directly. There had been no need to kill Salim. Just make him talk, and then he could have been kept out of the way. People do not often die in the hands of the police — not when the police want them alive. The professionals understand too well the techniques of persuasion and coercion. Well, he would see. He had promised Joachim that he would find out, and that was why he was here.

The engines on the two Panhards fired almost simultaneously, pushing clouds of blue exhaust across the dappled sunlit cobbles of the yard, then they trundled off down the long drive and the dust marked their progress beneath the eucalyptus. Two more took their place and the armourers moved in. The key turned in the door but Argand did not move, although his pulse quickened. Beneath the sharpness of Pérez's cologne he could now detect a sourness — tiredness, anxiety, fear? He made room for the large man to stand next to him at the window.

"You know there is to be a coup, a unilateral declaration of independence."

"I know that is what you hope for, what you are planning."

"Does Joachim know about this too? We think you spent last night in his apartment. The janitor says so, and the maid."

Argand detected . . . scorn? distaste? in Pérez's tone.

"I don't number law-breakers amongst my friends."

Pérez pushed that on one side. "Aren't you afraid we will kill you?"

"No. Why should you? If your plans are successful I shall no longer be a danger. If they are not then one more crime will only make your position worse."

"You do not expect them to be successful."

"No."

"Why not?"

162

Argand remained silent. Below, flighted mortar bombs, in cases of six, were being loaded into one of the new Panhards. One of the men stumbled, the case almost dropped. Argand wondered if the bombs had been armed, how well the people below knew what they were doing. Well, the legionaries should know, but he imagined the police, if that was what the others were, might not be so handy with them.

"Why not successful?" Pérez repeated. "Because your friend Joachim has informed the authorities?"

"He is not my friend."

"No. I do not think he can be. Do you know he has left Las Guavas? Left his wife here, left her with the body of her son still to be buried, in that apartment of theirs where you had supper last night?" Now Argand reacted — he had not realized that the body had been there all the time he had been talking with Joachim. Pérez detected what he hoped was weakness and went quickly on. "No doubt he hopes her British passport will protect her. Odd how older people still believe that that ostentatiously large affair with its royal coat of arms can still give some sort of extra protection to the holder — does he think the Queen will send a gunboat to get her out? But she won't even get past their immigration officers. Well, he seems not to care for her much so long as he is safe. So I imagine he's not much bothered with you. No. I don't think he has told the authorities. Why if he had should he have got the last plane out?"

Argand turned now and faced Pérez, whose eyes immediately flinched away. Beyond his shoulder the Infanta's smile seemed yet more serene as Argand repeated his words.

"The last plane out? You have closed the airport then?" Argand was sure that this was not the case. Joachim had told him that the airforce units that shared the airport facilities with the civil airlines, together with the garrison of mainland troops, would remain loyal to the Crown. He had decided that the safest place to give the alert from would be the airport. It sounded as if he had been right. Argand began to feel more sure of himself.

Pérez's reply was significantly equivocal: "The airport is closed."

"But not by you?"

Pérez shrugged. "It doesn't signify," he said. "Perhaps more blood will be spilled than would have been necessary. That is as much as you and Joachim will achieve." He felt in his pockets, fitted a cigarette into his short amber holder. "Tell me, Commissioner, just why did you come here?"

"To find out who killed Salim Robertson."

"Does it matter? Salim Robertson was caught between struggling forces. It does not matter who pulled the trigger — whoever it was was an agent of forces beyond his or Salim's control."

"There was no trigger. You know that very well. There were electrodes, burns from a cigarette, a garrotte. Other obscenities."

Pérez's lighter flared. "And bruises too. Around the mouth."

Argand turned away, back to the window. His fist tightened on the glass eye in his pocket. Down below Carlos had reappeared. He was shouting at the men, waving his arms, urging them to be quicker, to work harder. From his shoulder was slung a Heckler and Koch machine-pistol which he used like an extended limb to gesture with.

The voice came again in Argand's ear, the breath this time tainted with cigarette smoke.

"It's very important to you to know who killed Salim?"

Argand assented.

"If I tell you, will you do something for me?"

"If it is not illegal."

"Definitely not. Quite the reverse. Well?"

"I should think so. If it is reasonably within my power."

164

"Very well. That is your man. The one down there in the black beret, interfering with the armourers."

"I thought so."

"He is thought to be a bastard of my respected father-in-law." Argand remarked the distaste in Pérez's voice again.

"And what do you want me to do?"

"I want you to come to the centre of operations, which is here in the main rooms, and then stay there. I shall probably say that you have helped us, given me information I need."

"And then what?"

"Nothing. Simply stay there and observe. And later give the authorities a fair account of what happens. Especially of . . . my actions."

"The authorities."

"Yes." Pérez used his thumbnail to prise the unfinished cigarette from his holder. He flicked it out of the window. "You understand?"

"Yes. I understand."

XVIII

THE two largest rooms in the finca were separated by a removable partition. This had been opened to make one long hall. Moreover, the four French windows that gave access to the parterres where the barbecue had been held were also open — the consequence was that Salvador Guzmán's headquarters had an open spaciousness, a grandeur even, if one considered the view, not often available to conspirators as the moment of truth draws near.

The atmosphere was confused. At the opposing ends of this space it seemed that serious business was going forward. By the fireplace of what was normally the drawing-room, a radio transmitter and receiver had been set up, together with a field telephone, a conventional telephone, and a switch-board. Round these, a number of men — mostly young and some in uniform — were buzzing quietly and seriously; the talk was low, from time to time one with earphones would look up and signal to the others to be quiéter while he scribbled away on a pad. Then the paper would be torn off and carried briskly to the other end.

Here too things were serious. The handsome dining-room table was covered with maps, a small group of rather elderly gentlemen and ladies stood or sat around it, and the whole was dominated by the large nineteenth-century canvas, heavily framed — the painting of the four liberal revolutionaries who had faced the metropolitan firing squad by the seashore in 1832. Of the living beneath it, one stood out on account of the episcopal purple he was wearing, another because of his height, the ruin of his good looks, and the respect with which he was treated. It was to him that the messages from the other end were brought — Pérez's father-in-law, the putative first president of Las Virtudes, the bankrupt Salvador Guzmán.

Between these two ends and out on the terrace things were different. A large cold collation had been set out — carved chickens and pheasants, whole sliced bream and carp, jointed lobsters, hams and pâtés stood on white linen between banks of glasses, buckets of champagne and whisky bottles. As Argand, with Pérez behind him, moved further into the room, a cork popped and was greeted with a slight cheer and a renewed buzz of excited chatter. To Argand's amazement he recognized some of the faces in the group of twenty or so who were milling, somewhat aimlessly, around the tables. Many of them had been at the barbecue, yes, there were the two French scholars who had got so drunk, and was Françoise Brunot there too? He could not see her, but she was small. A spasm of alarm tinged with a less familiar emotion — tenderness? — jabbed like a needle. He turned to look for Pérez, turned to say — these people shouldn't be here, get these people away before they come to harm, and found himself face to face with, inevitably, the cherubic smile of Professor Shiner.

"Commissioner! We *do* seem destined to meet in unlikely circumstances."

Argand looked wildly around, but Pérez had gone, was standing now on the outskirts of the group around Guzmán, talking quietly to his wife, an attractive dark woman who yet had a look of the would-be president about her. She glanced down the room, prompted by something Pérez had said to her, looked in fact at Argand, and then turned back to her husband.

"It's all very exciting, I'm sure," Shiner continued. "Perhaps just a little too exciting. When you reach my age, and if I may say so, position . . ."

"But what are you doing here?" Argand exclaimed.

167

"It's all really too silly for words. There was going to be an *agasajo* . . ."

"A what?"

"A reception, don't you know. We were all to be here, and the chairman of the *Congreso* was to present a leather-bound example of the new edition of the Works to our host here. Then apparently it was cancelled, the *agasajo* I mean, but news of the cancellation was only passed on to the conference centre, the Casa de Colón, not to the *Residencia Universitaria*, so here we all are, all those of us who are staying there, that is."

"Then Dr Brunot is here?"

"Your fellow countrywoman? Can I say that? *Fellow*? Woman? Well, I have, so I can. Forgive me. It's the excitement. No, actually I think not. As you know she has scruples about this sort of thing. A feeling that she should no longer enjoy quite so flagrantly the fruits of the ruthless appropriation of the surplus value of the downtrodden . . . oh, I'm sure you know the sort of thing. Anyway she stayed at home. Actually she has still her paper to give, the day after tomorrow, so I expect she's just being a swot. Would you like a drink?"

Argand was again hungry. "I would like something to eat."

"Yes, well. So would I. But I'm not sure if all this is really meant for us. I rather gather it's to be the celebratory feast when our host is safely swathed in the imperial purple. However, I do see that one or two of my younger colleagues have availed themselves, so why not? Why not indeed? May I help you to a slice of this excellent-looking fish?"

"But why did they let you stay here? Why didn't they just take you all back down again?"

"Yes. Because no sooner had we arrived than some young whipper-snapper commandeered our bus to move some of our host's troops to some vantage point or other, and by the time that

168

had been sorted out we were in the know. So here we stay until it's all over. It doesn't augur well for the efficient running of the new country, does it? I mean, a balls-up like that right at the outset. That is if they pull if off." The little Scotsman was suddenly serious, head on one side. "Do you think, Commissioner, that they *will* pull if off?"

"No. I don't."

"No. Nor do I. As far as I can gather things have already gone against them at the airport. Oh dear. I hope that doesn't mean there's going to be some ghastly sort of show-down here, a *shoot-out*. I begin to wish I had shared some of our Dr Brunot's scruples against grinding the faces of the poor . . . This fish is excellent. I think we may as well eat and be merry after all."

He contrived to fork up a mouthful of bream with one hand while a colleague on his far side filled a glass with champagne for him.

"Not quite as chilled yet as I should have liked — perhaps we should have waited . . ."

As he spoke there was a stir at the far end of the room beneath the picture of the nineteenth-century liberals. Guzmán came round the table and stood facing them, the seven or eight men around him grouped themselves on either side — the bishop, or arch-bishop, was on his right, Pérez and Cortés amongst those on his left. A group portrait by Goya. "*Señores, se les pide, silencio para el primer presidente de las Virtudes,*" someone called, and others went shhhh and shush.

"My dear, I think he's going to make a speech," murmured Shiner, "indeed this may be the historical moment itself, the *pronunciamiento*. No doubt it will be repeated later on radio and island TV, but this is the one that counts . . . ." The room was now almost silent, and then, just as Guzmán was about to speak there was a slight movement behind him — his daughter's face

169

appeared briefly behind the archbishop, she touched Pérez's shoulder, Pérez looked down the hall at Argand, nodded, and then followed his wife out through a door behind the group. In front of them a photoflash briefly flared, throwing black shadows against the oak-lined walls behind, then Guzmán began. He spoke slowly, with much dignified gesture, and his voice took on an assumed sonority.

"*Amigos, Virtudianos, Compatriotas,*" he began. "*El Día más histórico de nuestras islas . . .*"

As he went on Shiner began to translate fragmentarily under his breath, and Argand bent slightly to catch the Scot's whisper.

"Servant of historical forces . . . the inevitable and indomitable resistance of a gallant island people . . . against the faceless monolithic giants of our times . . . we should use them, not be used by them . . . for this we need independence . . . Madrid bureaucrats the servants of the big corporations. A great power has chosen our island . . . part of a great defensive system against the godless rise of the most evil philosophy ever invented by corrupt and depraved men . . . as an independent people we will be able to play to the full the role destiny has assigned to us in the struggle against communism . . . but only with independence . . . the forces of socialism stalk again the *barrios* of the mainland cities . . . no disloyalty in what we are doing . . . the true spirit of Spain, of Sant'Iago, will be kept alive here like a pure flame, and from it, God willing, will be rekindled in mainland Spain . . . . Here, in Las Virtudes, we will once again be one nation, one society, not two. Our great countryman, our beloved Benítez, in his masterwork *The Two Nations*, first described the terrible split, the abyss brought about by greed on one side and arrogant presumption on the other . . . How noble, how right it is that here on Santa Caridad we should be the first people to incarnate the vision of that noble mind, bring back to our peoples the seamless unity . . ."

170

Argand's attention began to flag, and his eye wandered along the uneven line of faces that flanked the posturing, mouthing bankrupt in the centre. The bishop, whose pouchy half-hidden eyes flickered from floor to ceiling and almost never paused between; the banker, pushing out his lips, sucking in his cheeks, occasionally nodding or shaking his head slowly from side to side; a tall dark man in riding gear, with long hair beautifully cut to fall just across his immaculate velvet collar; a soldier with a grey face and a grey moustache above weak lips and a weaker chin — all were solemn, self-consciously solemn, playing their parts on an historical occasion but — yes, that was it — parts only, like actors on a stage, not like participants in an action, a real action, but running through an empty ritual that could well mean nothing at all. In short, all of them, Argand realized, were thinking of nothing but how they appeared, they were not really concerned with revolution, rebellion, or independence, or the people of Las Virtudes — what they were thinking about was how they looked, about their behaviour, about being sure that when they recalled this occasion from some as yet unknown future they would be able to say of themselves — yes, then, when Guzmán made his *pronunciamiento*, I was there, and I stood right, with the proper expression written on my face, as a hidalgo, the son of someone should. . . .'

"So, hand in hand, in blessed partnership, island capital and island labour, and island Church preserving the old liturgy, we will go forward into a glorious future, assisted by our friends across the sea, both in Spain and the United States, but never again dominated by them — *Adelante Isleñas*, *Adelante Virtudianos*, the future belongs to us!"

The applause was solid, dignified, interspersed with occasional *bravos* and *vivas*, more champagne corks popped and the chatter surged back, more excited, more frenetic than before.

"That went off rather well, don't you think?" murmured Shiner. "A fine old Hispanic tradition the *pronunciamiento*, you know, fallen into desuetude on this side of the Atlantic since 1936, so I suppose we should feel privileged to witness its revival. I only hope the occasion is as auspicious as our friend would have us believe, though I fear it won't be. I've a nasty feeling he's done it all prematurely because he feels he may not have the opportunity to do it at all later. In fact I think I'll have another drop of bubbly." And indeed, the radio operator from the other end of the room now brushed by, jogging his elbow. The expression on his young face was not merely anxious any longer, it was frightened.

The chatter became louder, tinged with hysteria. The food began to disappear, the conspirators now joining the uninvited guests from the *Congreso Beníteziano* in an almost orgiastic rush to get it all down while they still had the chance. Fingers took over from forks, chicken limbs, gobbets of fish and shellfish were thrust into the piquant sauces, crusty bread was crushed round cold meats into giant sandwiches and rammed between chomping jaws. Glass dropped and shattered, wine trickled from mouths and across cheeks and chins. Shiner drifted away, and then back again.

"Yes," he said to Argand, "it is bad news I'm afraid. They have an observer over at the barracks. The garrison is mobilizing. No doubt of it at all."

"They must have expected that."

"Perhaps. But not yet. Only in response to their first move which, I gather, was to be the occupation of the radio station and so on by the Legion in Las Guavas. But the Legion hasn't moved out of the port, and the garrison *is* coming out of the barracks. They're blown I'm afraid. Someone's ratted on them."

Joachim.

A helicopter clattered overhead. The people on the parterre

scattered beneath it, pushed back into the room. More glass fell, a table laden with trifles overturned.

"Not, I think," said Shiner, "one of ours."

But still nothing actually happened, not for another half hour at least, and manners, behaviour, appearances broke down further with each passing minute. Only three or four of Guzmán's associates remained with him, hedging him off from the riot; the Archbishop had withdrawn to say the Tridentine Mass and at the far end of the room three of the wireless and telephone operators still stuck to their posts though increasingly despairing of understanding what was coming through to them for the din around them.

In the meantime the party went on. The tables were soon scavenged clear if not clean, the last of the champagne was drunk and the whisky began to disappear too. Minor conspirators, hangers-on, became indistinguishable from scholars and academics, all milled together excitedly, drunkenly, the ones at the windows — few actually ventured on to the terraces now — shouting back to the rest what they had seen or thought they had seen in the hills beyond or the skies above. For a time the mood lightened — mortar fire, heavy machine-guns from four or five kilometres off were reported: yes, Pérez's men were resisting the approach of the garrison, of the regular army, after all; perhaps, who could say? all was not yet lost, and there was a surge to the parterre where those who had had some military training confidently interpreted the distant popping and clatter, the puffs of smoke and occasional flashes for those who had not. And in the middle of it all Argand noticed the young wireless operator suddenly white, deathly white as he strained at his earphones. Then, without a word he took them off, stood up, shrugged, and slipped away. This time whatever he had heard he was keeping to

173

himself. He went out by one of the french windows, and, by the time he had reached the end of the terrace and the path down to the yard beneath, he was trotting briskly.

This time the shooting was close, very close, and again the crowd pushed, trampled, and plundered its way back inside. Caught in it much as he had been at Barajas airport when he had first lost his case, Argand was suddenly disgusted to see he had trodden in a trifle or gâteau of some sort — his left foot was smirched with cream and jam. Shiner was at his elbow, pulling at his sleeve, and together they made their way to the back wall, between the fireplace and the painting, close to the door Pérez had vanished through before Guzmán had begun his speech, and as they got there Carlos, still in his combat gear, suddenly appeared through one of the centre windows. He was followed by three similarly dressed bravos, who, like him, flourished machine-pistols as if they were artificial limbs attached to the ends of their arms. Silence spread around them and Salim's murderer began to bark — orders, threats, menaces, Argand could not make out a word.

"Oh dear," said Shiner. "Don't move. He says he'll shoot the next one of us to move. He has already shot the wireless operator who was trying to escape. We are to stay still, and when the time comes we are to fight, fight to the last drop . . . for Las Virtudes, for President Guzmán . . . I'm very much afraid this man is mad, homicidally so."

His speech finished, Guzmán's bastard came down the room towards them, his head swinging wildly as he tried to keep the whole area under the scrutiny of his one eye, but when he reached Guzmán his face relaxed into a twisted smile, he flung his free arm round the failed revolutionary's shoulders and clumsily bear-hugged him before turning back to face the rest of the room. Again he spoke, his voice softer, but still fervent, urging, exhorting,

174

appealing, the Heckler and Koch swinging and jabbing to emphasize his points, while with his left arm he continued to hug his presumed father. From his place behind Argand could see only the black eye-patch, the black beret, and the wildly jerking gun. In front of him the crowd, rabble now, had fallen almost silent, white-faced, and suddenly sober in the face of this insane Nemesis. At Argand's side Shiner still clung, but silent too, no longer prepared to risk drawing attention to himself by interpreting what the assassin had to say.

At this point Pérez entered, through the door to Argand's left, beyond Guzmán and the rest. He made little noise but his purpose was plain — to Argand at least, for the police-chief carried a Walther P38, and there were three similarly armed policemen behind him: he had come to arrest his father-in-law and thus make his peace with the authorities they had briefly defied, and he wanted Argand there as an independent witness to this final act of loyalty to the Crown. But clearly he did not know what had happened in his absence, did not know how the killer with the eye-patch had taken control of the room, was threatening any traitor with instant execution.

As Pérez began the formal statement of arrest several things happened almost at once. First, distant, but rapidly increasing in volume, came the scream of airborne jets. Simultaneously Argand extricated from his pocket the eight-inch solid cylinder the Basque had thrust on him; he shouted, and hurled it at Carlos who was at that moment twisting towards Pérez, using Guzmán as a shield, and levelling his machine-pistol at the police-chief's stomach. The cylinder caught him glancingly on the side of the head, he hesitated for a second and then swung back, his head lurching as he strove to bring his good eye round to bear on this new threat from his blind side. And the machine-pistol came round with his head, was firing, spewing out bullets before it was anywhere near aimed. Argand felt Shiner plucked away from his side as if by a sudden gale, then the searing burn as a bullet pecked at the top part of his own arm; Pérez's gun fired too, and the machine-pistol's burst stuttered to a standstill as the finger on its trigger straightened in a death spasm.

Pandemonium broke out beyond, but the sounds of terror were erased by the scream of the jets above, only hundreds of metres above, as three Phantom F4-Cs went by, wiping out all other noise, however loud, as completely as a damp blackboard eraser obliterates marks on a chalky blackboard.

The Phantoms were followed by the deeper roar of turbo-props. Shiner choked and then drowned in his own blood. Argand cradled the Professor's head across his knees and failed to mark how the sky had filled with a daisy-chain of parachutes which floated down a lazy, twisting parabola towards the shambles below.

XIX

FRANÇOISE Brunot mounted the podium, adjusted the height of the lectern which reached her chin, ran her hand briefly down the front of her dress, and began. Her voice was high and clear, her Spanish immaculately Castilian.

"My eminent colleagues have paid their last respects on behalf of us all to a great scholar and a kind, good gentleman. It is not now for me to add to what they have said, indeed it would be presumptuous of me to do so. The greatest compliment I can pay the memory of Professor Shiner is to deliver the lecture I have prepared, conscious though I am, indeed conscious *as* I am that he would have disapproved and challenged almost all I am about to say. To do this is to compliment his memory, and not to show it disrespect, not simply because he would have wished me to do so, but because he was a liberal who still contrived to cling to some of the values of the defunct tradition of liberal humanism. Not the least of these is a belief in the sanctity of free discourse, of lively, untrammelled intellectual activity, without fear of where thought might lead, challenging the intolerance of those whose prejudices and own fears have closed their minds to new ideas.

"Mr Chairman, my subject this morning is *Las Dos Naciones*, and its critics. *The Two Nations* is above all the book on which we place our claim that Jorge Benítez should be numbered amongst the great critical realists of the nineteenth century, Balzac, Dickens and Tolstoy. But this claim is meaningless for as long as we continue to give that work readings and explications which bleed from it every drop of its life-blood, that is that deny it the truly critical element in its make-up.

"That such readings are currently the norm goes without saying. I need only refer you to Professor Salas's latest consideration of the closing chapters, which, according to him, present a picture of reconciliation and hope based on a frankly reactionary view of society as unchanging, hierarchical, and committed to the preservation of private property.

"To counter effectively rubbish of this sort a new methodology is needed. And before I move on to the work we are considering I would like briefly to outline some of the assumptions on which I think such a new methodology may be based . . ."

"Well, hell, you sure did fuck up the whole enterprise when you lifted poor Salim's case at Barajas. That was a neat move Commissioner, a very neat move."

The prickling sensation behind his ears, the sudden heat in his palms, Argand had not experienced these since he had, he thought, seen through it all in Joachim's apartment. But now . . . what was this? What was this untidy, gauche American saying now? He paused, forced Peters to a standstill too, while he awkwardly wiped his brow with his left hand. His right arm was still bound up in a small black sling.

He looked out over the last still unspoilt piece of earth for many hectares. Below them the trucks roared down the rough carriageways with their loads of conglomerate, and bulldozers continued to nudge plantations, fences, and irrigation channels from side to side until they fell apart. Much of the plant still carried the blazon San Salvador SA, and why not? No doubt politenesses would be observed, delicacies even, in boardrooms, law courts, churches, drawing-rooms, and officers' messes, but out here no one was going to lose expensive plant time while the name of a bankrupt traitor was scrubbed off the panelling.

"A neat move. Put us right there on the spot. Of course. I made it easy for you."

Argand contrived an expression of polite enquiry. Behind the sling his heart began to pound, and he felt sick.

"Sure, I made it easy. Hell, how was I to know? Salim had to get the stuff in a case. Those Pandore things were lying all over the EUROSTRUCT offices, they'd bought in five hundred of them as gifts, handouts, perks. So naturally you had the twin of Salim's case." He laughed — an awkward, rasping sound. Then he walked on, kicking the tufa like a spoiled boy who has been robbed of some minor prize by a piece of bad luck. Argand had time to collect his wits, to remember too something Joachim had said.

He caught up with the American. "Yes, but why heroin?"

"And not gems? The way Joachim wanted it? Well, the South African boys let us down there. Maybe, after doing a lot of the spadework for us uncovering Joachim's organization they just felt turning the whole deal into a way of financing a coup, where they had no direct interest, just wasn't worth the candle. Hell, I don't know. But what I do know is there was I stuck in Amsterdam with nothing to give Salim and twenty-four hours to find something. Then our Drug Law Enforcement boys just happened to bust a ring in one of our Rhineland bases and we were up to our ankles in the stuff. Seemed too good to be true. And one of them owed me a favour so I was able to pesuade him to lend me three kilos." Peters paused, turned, his grey eyes cool behind the glasses, his head tilted slightly to one side so the skin on the upper cheek was drawn tight while that on the other creased over his collar. "It was a loan, Commissioner. I'd like to have the stuff back. Have you any idea what came of it?"

But Argand pushed the whereabouts of the heroin to the back of a mind that had jumped connections to the real heart of it all. The Americans, some Americans at any rate, had wanted their Base on Santa Caridad, the boss of the Shield of Achilles, removed from

Spanish, European influence, wanted it held by a government that depended on them, on dollars alone, for its existence.

What Peters said next proved him right.

"I've not yet figured out just who you are working for. I mean your cover here, this business of advising IBOBRAS on security is absolutely bloody watertight, I mean it is what you're doing, right? I really did not cotton on to you until after that little Pakistani runt had snuffed it without saying anything more about the horse than that you had taken it and hidden it. Well, Jesus, that was no accident."

Argand stopped, looked at the American with cold eyes, and his voice was cold too.

"Were you there when Salim died?"

Peters seemed not to sense any particular urgency in Argand's voice. "Hell, no. I left all that to Guzmán's boys. But they reported him accurately, I'm sure. So. Right at the start I was on to you. We kept tracks. You sent in an info-request to CRIC — you were up to something, on to something, but how much did you know? Carlos found nothing in your room and then you put me right back to square one by recommending we had the Legion in for the digger. Well you couldn't be trying to bust the coup after that. You had to be clean. I reckon that was your neatest move of all, that was a card I wouldn't call."

Argand turned away. What to say, what to say to this absurd and evil man. A rare smile twitched in the corner of his mouth — at least he was not alone in suffering from paranoid fantasies. Clearly Peters had to believe that his conspiracy had failed because something big and powerful had been working against him.

"And you won't tell me now, between friends, who you're working for? Of course not. Well, there are all sorts of new Euro-agencies springing up, we'll get wise to them as time goes on. Hell, I can understand the feeling in Bonn or Brussels — you Euros like the idea of the Shield of Achilles, but you want to keep a piece of it, right? If Las Virtudes slips out of your sphere of influence how can you be sure Uncle Sam will activate when the Russkies cross the Elbe? I get the point. But we have a point too. Look what we lost in Iran. Is Juan Carlos any better fixed than the Shah was? I've heard it said he might yet turn out to be the first constitutional monarch with a commie Prime Minister. Swell for him, but it sure would make the boss of our Shield of Achilles look like a leaky kettle."

He turned and spat, rubbed the gum, match-stalk or whatever into the black dust, then looked up over the spoiled earth, through the shimmering heat, towards the high rises that marked the outskirts of Las Guavas. "Not long now," he said.

Argand looked at his watch. "Not long," he agreed.

"Let me sum up the argument so far." Françoise looked out over the sea of moonish faces beneath the beautiful coffered ceiling of the main lecture hall. Columbus had spread his maps in this room, discussed the movement of the stars with the monks from San Cristóbal — even then the clear air had made study of the heavens above Santa Caridad a more reliable business than in most other places. "I have shown how each of the three dominant interpretations of the end of *Las Dos Naciones* over the hundred years of its existence has in its own way more to tell us of the time in which it was made than of the book it purports to illuminate, and I have suggested that the determining force in each case was the dominant ideology of the time. And this is so in spite of the fact that the critics were working with what we still say was the same text.

"Now Professor Shiner took as a *donné* the text as something pure, fixed, and final, and the aim of criticism the discovery of a once and for all, final truth about that text. The thrust of my argument is that this simply will not do. Granted, and we all do grant it, that the text is more than black marks on white paper, we must develop an altogether more subtle and complex idea of just what a text is.

"What I am proposing to you, taking *Las Dos Naciones* as my example, is that a text always and only exists in a variety of historically concrete forms in the midst of concrete and changing determinants which condition the ways in which it is appropriated during its history . . ."

Below, in the courtyard, the parrot screamed.

"What *is* that smell?" It took Argand back three nights to when he had stood waiting in the odorous dark for the bus. Now it was stronger than ever, and not mingled with the scent of flowers. Peters passed behind him, unwrapped a stick of gum.

"Like randy tomcats?" he asked. "You've been a week on Santa Caridad and you don't know that smell yet?" He reached up and pulled a fruit from the tree they were under. It was yellowish green, looked like a nobbly pear. He pulled it open and the smell became a stink. "Guava. Surprised, eh? They only get like this when they're a bit overripe." His voice pleaded again. "Commissioner, what about the horse, the heroin?"

Argand looked out over the plain. Two Sikorsky helicopters were now buzzing over the city that took its name from this unpleasant fruit.

"I believe the commander of the Civil Guard has it. It was found at Guzmán's finca."

"Well, he won't know where it came from."

Argand breathed a deep sigh. "No. Not yet."

"Not yet?"

Argand shaded his eyes. On the edge of the town they could now see swirling lights, blue and yellow, just beneath the helicopters.

Peters swore slowly and steadily and very obscenely for a minute or more. Argand tried not to listen. However, when the stream of filth had stopped he assented to what had been meaningful in it — that Peters was right to suppose that Argand saw it as his duty to tell the Spanish authorities where the heroin had come from.

The American apparently had nothing else to say to him. He turned on his heel and stumped away down the slope towards the black Mercedes where Pérez's successor waited to take them back to the entrance to the site. Argand followed. He felt pleased about the heroin; as soon as he had learnt where it came from he had decided that he would obstruct its return to whatever agency it was Peters worked for. Such people, Argand believed, were not to be trusted with stuff as potentially harmful as *horse*.

Françoise paused, took a sip of water. Not long to go, she thought — and at least they've heard me out. I rather thought they might not.

"What therefore I am urging on you is the abandonment of the fixed text as given, and the acceptance in its place of the essential instability of texts, with the awareness that this instability is not, as the liberal humanist tradition would like us to believe, a function of the greatness of a text, that is that the concomitant of its universality, completeness and complexity is that it can support a diversity of contradicting interpretations at the same time, but that this diversity is a function of the text's instability, and that this instability is historically determined.

"Granted this, what then? Well, it becomes evident that the enterprise of criticism can be seen clearly as a political undertaking, a series of interventions within and struggles for the uses to which texts are to be put. From the black marks on white paper that are the only stable things about *Las Dos Naciones* we may now set about creating texts that will take up positions within the field

183

of cultural relations which will actively assist rather than obstruct the broader social process. Only by frankly and consciously adopting such a position will we be able effectively to counter the appropriation of this text, and indeed the whole *oeuvre* of Benítez by the educational apparatus of the Christian Democrat state Spain is today. *Señores, nada más!*"

The reception was low-keyed — perhaps because a mood of mourning still pervaded the fourth Benítezian Congress in Las Guavas, perhaps because the majority of the audience had not understood more than a quarter of what she had been trying to say.

She looked across the sea of faces and her heart sank. First on his feet, waving his programme, was the thin grey figure of the French structuralist.

"I should like to ask," he began, in a thin dry voice, "to what extent Dr Brunot accepts post-Saussurian analyses of polysemanticity as valid tools for the sort of ongoing project she has in mind for *Las Dos Naciones* and to what extent and why she rejects or accepts the methodological implications of Derrida's deconstruction theory . . ."

At the entrance to the site a few hundred pickets, still bravely displaying some of the banners of three days before, waited in sullen silence facing a double line of paratroopers. They were there in defiance of the state of emergency that had been declared following the attempted coup, and consequently they risked at the least summary arrest and detention. And they knew the troops could fire without fear of reprimand. With the helicopters above it, under its umbrella of black fumes, and flanked by more soldiers in troop carriers, the giant heap of machinery that would cut the trench for the mobile rocket launchers, inched its way slowly towards them. Amongst them was the Basque who had talked with Argand on the way down from the university residence. The sight

184

of the foreign policeman now in the Mercedes that cruised by on its way to meet the digger spiced the little man's despair with bitterness but not surprise. The dour Brabanter Commissioner was a hero now, so the media said. He had saved them all from fighting in the streets, civil war. Ah, thought the Basque, shaking his Cro-Magnon head, they're all the same, they're all in it. None of them really knows or understands the madness they've got us all into. He turned away, pushed his way out of the small crowd. Suddenly the noise and smell of the advancing juggernaut was too much for him.

Françoise Brunot bundled her papers together, and looked at the backs of the last of the *congresistas* leaving the hall in front of her. She felt flat, dispirited. She wished now she had cancelled her lecture, had gone instead to picket the Base. In this blank moment she had no illusions about why she had not done so — she did not try to persuade herself that her lecture was important, would do more to forward the things she believed in. She had not done so because she was frightened, frightened now, as she had not been in May '68, of paratroopers with orders to shoot, of baton charges and mace. There was another thing too — in the world of Benítezian scholarship it is an important thing to give a lecture at a plenary session of the Congress, no denying it, that had been a consideration.

"*Hola,*" cried the parrot, as she descended the open staircase into the muggy warm daylight. "*¿Qué tal? Hola, muy bien gracias.*"

185

XX

AFTERWORD

"YOUR chap Argand did very well in the Virgin Islands."

"*Virtue* Islands, sir." Secretary Prinz sucked complacently on his pipe. The smoke swirled and then eddied towards the round shiny face of the English Eurocrat who co-ordinated internal security projects in Brussels.

"He'd been ill, I believe."

"Quite recovered now, I'm glad to say. Did him good to get away."

"The Spaniards are very pleased with us, very pleased. And the Yanks have egg on their faces. Always a good idea. Of course they think we sent your chap in with just that in mind."

Prinz narrowed his eyes, tried to penetrate the fog he had created between them. Had there been just a hint of query in the Eurocrat's voice?

"No harm in letting them think that, is there, sir?"

"No, not at all. None at all. They'll think twice before they meddle in our patch again, eh? At least let us know what they're up to."

Prinz sucked away.

But the Eurocrat still felt that he too had perhaps been left a touch underinformed.

"Seconded to IBOBRAS, wasn't he?"

"That's right."

"And they're tied in with EUROSTRUCT. Big business, EURO-STRUCT."

"Very."

"Do you suppose . . .?"

"You mean . . .?"

"Well they tend to know what they're doing."

Prinz stopped puffing, knocked filthy ashes into the Eurocrat's ashtray. He could see that if he wasn't careful it would appear that he, at any rate, had *not* known what he was doing.

He straightened and smiled boldly.

"Of course IBOBRAS knew that Guzmán was up to something. His affairs were very shaky indeed — he *had* to be up to something. . . ."

"So you're saying they, as it were, *injected* Argand into the situation."

Prinz's smile became grateful. "Something like that, sir."

"Well, that's all right then." The Eurocrat ran a podgy palm across his immaculate blotter, always a sign the interview was almost over. "I suppose your Argand will be back soon? Got something more lined up for him, have you? I must say he does seem a useful sort of chap. A bit wasted in a routine post like public order."

Prinz frowned, in spite of himself. What *was* he going to do with the Honest Commissioner? He'd have to think of something.